IN THE CHAIR SAT THE LATE PROFESSOR ARTHUR HALLAM.

There could be no doubt that he was dead; nobody could be that extraordinary colour and still live. On the screen above the podium, a bird of prey held in its claws the curved agonised body of a rabbit.

"And what does that mean?" Inspector Hunt asked.

"'Nature red in tooth and claw,'" Dr. Faraday quoted. "That's the first thing that came to my mind. It's a quotation from something or other. Mr. Baird here could place it for you."

"Or Mr. Roberts? Mr. Roberts is a dab hand at contexts, isn't he?" asked Inspector Hunt.

Mr. Roberts raised a pale face. "Oh, that's an easy one, Inspector. Any schoolboy doing English A Level would get it. It's from Tennyson's 'In Memoriam.'"

"An elegy," Baird explained, with a concerned glance for Mr. Roberts. "Tennyson wrote it for a friend of his called—oh, God!—called Arthur Hallam!"

Also by Edward Candy
Published by Ballantine Books:

BONES OF CONTENTION

WORDS FOR
MURDER PERHAPS

Edward Candy

BALLANTINE BOOKS • NEW YORK

Bantwich, as I have pointed out elsewhere, is an imaginary city, and can therefore have no university and, alas, no Extra-mural Department; and the staff and students of those two institutions must be imaginary too, although I would like to think some of them are not.

Library of Congress Catalog Card Number: 82-45965

ISBN 0-345-31952-4

This edition published by arrangement with Doubleday & Company, Inc.

Manufactured in the United States of America

First Ballantine Books Edition: January 1985

For Bill and Sheila Forster

CHAPTER ONE

Autumn in these islands is attended by a diversity of natural phenomena, some much celebrated by poets and painters: mists and mellow fruitfulness come to mind, and the rich colouring of certain Constable landscapes. The gathering swallows twitter for us much as they did for Keats, and generations of naturalists watch and record their departure and the arrival of geese and waxwings. School uniforms that fitted in the spring when they went to the cleaners fit no longer; joints begin, as yet mildly, to ache. Youthful bodies lose their suntan, girls wear more, men hope for less, and hot buttered toast for tea on Sundays spells sensual bliss for simple souls. Souls less simple feel clocks chiming all around them, even inside them, as the leaves flutter down in profuse negation of a love of order, blurring all decent distinction between lawn and flower bed, pavement and gutter. This is the season of regret for opportunities wasted, much more productive than the new year of good resolutions, of the desire to better oneself, to make something of life before it is too late. By the end of September or early October the doors of suburban houses open after the evening meal and men and women steal or spring forth according to temperament; more women actually than men, older persons rather than younger, but plenty of men all the same and quite a sprinkling of the

1

young. They are bound for the school buildings of the neighbourhood where they will paint or cook or sew or practise Russian conversation or play the guitar or keep fit or brush up their shorthand. Among them are a few whose plans for self-improvement are loftier, extending to the things of the mind. In big cities these few make for the Extra-mural Departments of universities; they have studied brochures and selected courses, they have filled in forms and made out cheques. They understand that they will be required to read certain books as well as attend a certain number of lectures, that they will be invited to contribute to discussions, perhaps even to submit written work. Some are old hands, have enrolled for such courses for years past, even for two or three courses at a time; they look upon the Extra-mural Department as home away from home, choose their subjects on what they have heard of the personality of the lecturer, look forward to the coffee break halfway through the evening and a chat with other habitués, regard newcomers with faint hostility concealed under bland words of welcome and advice on where to hang one's hat and coat.

In Bantwich, where the university was founded immediately after the First World War, the Extra-mural Department opened only two years later and is consequently one of the oldest in the country. It owes its existence to the foresight and philanthropy of the second most powerful industrial dynasty of the neighbourhood. The most powerful of all, the Bannister family, put their surplus into hospitals and dispensaries. The Snettisloes, finding the body well taken care of by their rivals, decided to purchase spiritual salvation by the appropriate means of providing sustenance for the spirits of their employees, and endowed the infant university with halls of residence, playing fields, prizes, and libraries. Finally they handed over their town house, known as the Chambers, whose value had declined sharply with the outward spread of the shopping centre, and retreated to their country place known as Snettisloe Grange. There is still a Snettisloe living, I believe, in Bermuda or Crete or Florence, somewhere at any rate cleaner than Bantwich, and certainly warmer in the year's decline.

To the Extra-mural Department in the Chambers, Sparks Lane, came consequently one October evening some of those generally saddened but not yet hopeless people beloved of Dr. Bentley, warden of Chambers, of Mervyn Prothero, his deputy, Miss Angus, their joint assistant, the librarian Humphrey Baird, and Christie Carr, his faithful helper; these, together with a tutor in each of the recognised branches, constituted the full time permanent academic and administrative staff of the department. The handsome double doors swung wide, admitting bearable draughts of temperate air, it was still daylight in the mean streets, the term was new-born. Later would come frost, sleet, snow, fog. A few of the faithful would continue to push against the doors come December, but many would prefer their own firesides after a day in classroom or office, at the bench or over the sink. And who could blame them? Mr. Roberts asked rhetorically of Mervyn Prothero, when the deputy warden brought him the registration sheet with twenty-four names typed down the page and subdivisions into weeks across. A wider column for entry of occupation drew both men's attention: housewife, teacher, teacher, clerk, housewife, clerk, clerk, civil servant, sales assistant, teacher, teacher, housewife, religious, religious, teacher, housewife, pharmacist (retired).

"There are no surprises," Prothero said. "Twenty-two of your lot are women and fifteen are over forty. One of the under-forties is a nun, so she hardly counts. Sometimes I feel sorry for you, Roberts, but perhaps you would be disconcerted if a pretty girl came and sat in the front row. Perhaps it would put you off your stroke."

Mr. Roberts smiled and felt uncomfortable. Mervyn Perthero was a bachelor and assumed that Mr. Roberts must be one, too, on no better grounds than that the only Mrs. Roberts known to himself was the man's mother, and no wife had ever presented herself at the Christmas Dance or Founders' Dinner. But the younger Mrs. Roberts was as real a person as the elder, though she had long ago become Mrs. Something Else. On numerous occasions Mr. Roberts had attempted to shake Prothero's high confidence. "We old bachelors—" was the deputy warden's common way of beginning some mildly silly statement of a position Mr. Roberts felt no wish to seem to share; a disclaimer would have come easily to most men, but Mr. Roberts shrank from seeming to wish to dissociate himself from Prothero, from seeming to administer a snub, however slight. He occupied countless similar false positions of which he was entirely ignorant, ranging from the role of perfect provider for his widowed mother, who actually had a substantial income of her own, to poet *manqué* on the strength of two contributions to *New Writing* in its heyday, that outburst of creativity coinciding in fact with the delayed breaking of his voice and the first blurring of down upon his upper lip. So much of his life was spent upon the verge of a disavowal that he had begun by forty to see ordinary candour as likely to be suicidal: a leap over the precipice on whose edge he might be allowed to teeter some years longer by the strenuous practice of suppressing all evidence of his real, indisputable, unbearable self. Experience told him that, by the end of term, two or three of the kind, plump ladies in his class would have ascertained the size of his feet and bought or knitted him socks for Christmas: how could he reveal himself as an unscrupulous exploiter of feminine goodwill, a man whose dressing chest concealed a wardrobe of socks adequate to a monstrous centipede, when the knowledge would only show up these good souls as fussy, officious, thoughtless providers of articles unwanted, unsolicited, positively a glut upon the market? Mr. Roberts read through his list therefore with no feeling of disappointment. A pretty girl would not have embarrassed him a jot, he considered, unless he caught her surreptitiously eyeing his shoes. In this, as in much else, he was mistaken.

"Here comes Humphrey with your books," Prothero now said, and Humphrey Baird came into Lecture Room Three with a porter staggering exaggeratedly under the weight of a metal-bound wooden box. "Better check the list before the class arrives. We had a bit of trouble tracing that article on the influence of Poe on Hoffmann—or was it Hoffmann on Poe? Anyway, it wasn't in Martin's book, it was in Hadfield's. You might check your references a little more thoroughly next time, old chap."

Mr. Roberts murmured an apology, because this seemed less difficult than to recall sentence by sentence a conversation he and Prothero had had in June, when he had attributed the article to Hadfield and the deputy warden, waggling an admonitory finger, had assured him that Martin, Martin of Leeds and now Wadham, was in fact the author. He reckoned without honest Humphrey Baird, who was concerned to preserve neither Prothero's good opinion of himself nor Roberts' defensive cloak of invisibility. "Rob said it was in Martin's book all along. You had an *idée fixe* about Hadfield, for some reason. The man never made a useful contribution about work of that period that I know of: early Gothic novels, that was his field. I've looked out his book an Bage and Godwin, by the way, Roberts; it wasn't on your list, but it's a good little thing of its kind."

Mr. Roberts was properly grateful: he had much to be grateful for, he now discovered. No less than three of the ladies whose names were on the new register had attended his last year's course on Defoe, Fielding, Richardson and Smollett. He had revealed to them the birth pangs of the English novel, had guided them through Defoe's gamey London into Fielding's generous fresh pastures; had attempted to explain to them, as well as to himself, Lovelace's deathless charm, that radiance of corruption which Mr. Roberts' own life had taught him to recognise as constituting for some women, if not for Clarissa Harlowe, the greatest of all possible attractions. He had noted anew, and with regret, the engrained distaste women feel for a robust ribaldry as he tried to arouse their enthusiasm for *Roderick Random* and *Peregrine Pickle*. And at the end of the course, when he felt in need of a holiday and they, poor souls, were finding more and better reasons for staying away, though by then it was March, the evenings light again and even sunny, he had read them a few pages of *Tristram Shandy*. They did not find my Uncle Toby amusing.

So this year, instead of tracing the novel through to maturity in the work of Jane Austen, Thackeray, Dickens and George Eliot, he had sidestepped recklessly in pursuit of a favourite topic of his own. "Not the history of the detective story," he had explained to the assembled Courses Committee, "I quite see that that would be too narrow altogether."

"And possibly too frivolous," Dr. Bentley had said, tapping on the leather top of the table before him. "At a time like this when we have to keep an eye, a very close eye, on our critics, is it wise, would you say, to set a precedent for studying—forgive me, Roberts!—a very doubtful minor genre? I merely ask, I merely wish to ascertain the general opinion."

Mr. Roberts would have abandoned his project then and there and settled for *Emma* and *Vanity Fair* as he had done every alternate year for some time past, but he had found an unexpected and, truth to tell, unwanted champion in Mervyn Prothero.

"Critics be damned, Bentley, if by critics you mean those wretched cheese-paring Philistines who think all our courses should be vocational, God help us! What's a department like this for, can anyone tell me"—and he turned fierce little reddish-brown eyes on his colleagues—"if not to lift people out of their everyday rut? All right, so we don't help them to do their jobs a little bit better, or earn a little more, or be rather more conscientious servants of our ghastly masters; but at least we offer them a chance to broaden their outlook, at least we offer them a glimpse of wider horizons."

"I am not perfectly sure," Dr. Bentley had then said, "that detective stories broaden or widen anything in particular except possibly one's knowledge of very dubious practices among the criminal classes. I am not in fact aware that the claim has ever been advanced for them that they tend to enhance their readers' appreciation of the finer things of life. I simply wonder, I simply would like to be informed upon this point."

"Roberts made no such claim." Prothero had been brisk, so brisk that Roberts' own disclaimer died on his lips. "He is offering something new, something fresh, something entirely nonutilitarian. Obviously that is bound to arouse misunderstanding and resentment among the mean and narrow-minded."

Mr. Roberts flinched, but Dr. Bentley declined to wear the cap so aggressively offered him. Magnanimity shone on his ample brow and Mr. Roberts was reminded of a great heavy dog, say a Newfoundland or a St. Bernard, turning off the yapping attacks of a toy poodle with maddening good temper.

"Narrow was the very word Roberts used, if I remember rightly, to deprecate the title suggested for the course. Not 'The History of the Detective Story,' he said. Perhaps he will tell us what title he would favour?"

"'Crime Fiction, Past and Present,'" Prothero said, while Mr. Roberts was clearing his throat, "and a splendid title, too, I call it. Ought to attract young people, a title like that. And if they come for crime fiction, they might stay for something more demanding. They might find themselves drawn in."

"The technique," Dr. Bentley said, with thorough sweetness, "is widely employed in supermarkets, I am told. It is called the loss leader. No reference to Browning is intended." Nobody laughed; the warden showed a little human disappointment by a gentle sigh. "Perhaps Roberts has not thought of himself as supplying a loss leader?"

Mr. Roberts had not, and now four months later as he recognised the name of the faithful, and observed under Prothero's guidance the general composition of the class, he was moved to remark that the manager of a supermarket must put quite a lot of thought into choosing which goods should be humiliatingly crammed into wire baskets near the entrance of his store. "I had the same number last year when the title was 'Some Early Ventures in English Narrative Prose,'" he said. "I did think 'Crime Fiction, Past and Present' had more panache, I must say."

"Never mind," Humphrey Baird said kindly. "Your soul is obviously above the level of cheap advertisement. Prothero is basically a vulgarian, for all the antidemocratic talk; we ought to get him to dream up titles for you. Could we get a course X-certificated, do you think?"

"Only over Dr. Bentley's dead body. But I won't despair just yet. There are always some last-minute registrations on the first night."

He sat down behind the long bench and studied his fingernails as twenty-two of his designated twenty-four students came in, mostly one at a time and shyly, but a few in groups, with conversation. The young nun was accompanied by an elderly one with a scrubbed pink face, a teacher from a famous convent school in the heart of the city, whose physical resemblance to anyone's notion of the Wife of Bath had left other lecturers besides Mr. Roberts with vague unformulated questions. The young one had thicker ankles than Sister Marie Louise: how strange, he thought, that he should have lived to know beyond all doubt that nuns actually had legs and did not, as his childhood self had taken for granted, propel themselves on small concealed wheels.

There was laughter, there were controlled and ladylike whoops of pleasure at the sight of him. Mrs. Berg, Mrs. Landor and Miss Blount came in hard on the visible heels of the two nuns and greeted him with friendly enquiries as to the success of his holiday and gay accounts of their own. He expressed gratification at their return to his classes, they assured him that they wouldn't have missed this course for the world, they were dying to know which books he recommended for their reading list, was Dennis Wheatley a prescribed author? Mr. Roberts said tactfully that perhaps they would come to Mr. Wheatley in due course, the first term's lectures would be concerned with the early development of the novel of suspense and mystification, by Christmas they would probably be tackling *The Mystery of Edwin*

Drood. Three eager faces fell; Miss Blount however brightened up again at once and she went happily to her place, remarking that Edwin Drood, now, was a really solid writer who could show these moderns a thing or two. Mr. Roberts made rapid efforts at calculation and came up with the remarkable figure of eighty-seven for Miss Blount's age, basing his sums on various hints dropped relating to the Boer War, the Diamond Jubilee and lovely garden parties in the grounds of Snettisloe Grange at the turn of the century when she was just a young thing and the weather was invariably sunny. Then he became aware that a young thing stood at his side, seemingly in the custody of Miss Angus, whose sturdy hand propelled her forward.

"Here's a latecomer, Mr. Roberts. Doesn't know what course she wants, thinks she'll give yours a try. What's your name, child?"

"Jones."

"First name?"

"Nan, Nancy."

"N. Jones, Miss," Miss Angus said, in fierce tones. The ferocity meant nothing.

"Mrs.," the young thing said, not shyly.

"Mrs. N. Jones. Write it down, Mr. Roberts. Goodness, it isn't a difficult name, Jones! Can't make any mistake spelling that, shouldn't think."

Miss Angus went out snorting. Mr. Roberts could not look at Mrs. Jones, who had witnessed his discomfiture at the older woman's hands, who knew on the spot and instantaneously what sort of man this was who, confronted with her beauty at this time and in this place, allowed his ballpoint to tremble contemptibly at the foot of the register before writing what Miss Angus had so efficiently dictated.

"Occupation?" he next asked in a stifled voice, and had to repeat it, on encountering her blank gaze.

"Oh, I don't know. What do you suggest?"

"You must know what your occupation is," he said, mustering courage.

"I know what I do all day. Nothing, really."

"Shall I put housewife?"

"Have you any others?"

He turned the register round, and she looked down the list. He seized his chance and looked at her, more fully than he had yet dared. She was not as young as he had thought, nor was she as beautiful. And a good thing, too, Mr. Roberts felt, in my circumstances.

"Housewife will do," she said. "Shall I write down my address?"

"Thank you, yes."

The address surprised him. The houses in that area were large, detached, the gardens big and well kept, some had swimming pools. Mr. Jones must be a man of substance to live there, a successful young businessman very likely, strident and pushing. But wouldn't the wife of such a man be more likely to spend her evenings at cocktail parties or in expensive restaurants? Mr. Roberts' imagination foundered; what did the rich do in Bantwich on Tuesday evenings between seven-thirty and nine? He thought it unlikely that they came and listened to refugees from the hurly-burly of the university's English Department riding their hobby horses for a few guineas a time.

"I must start with an apology," he shortly began, for she had taken herself off to a seat at the back, a bad sign: in his experience those who sat at the back rarely came two weeks running. The eager beavers would be in the front rows, where they could catch his eye during those fiercely happy discussion periods that followed the coffee break; when every question he put forward, Mr. Roberts well knew, no matter how lucid the wording, would produce an answer calculated to confound all rational argument, and every opinion given would release inevitably a flood of personal doubt and disturbance, ultimately relating to the length of young people's hair, promiscuity, drugs and the rights of squatters.

Mr. Roberts made, then, his apology. He had felt, he told them, that simply to proceed chronologically with the mainstream development of the English novel—worthwhile though such a project would undoubtedly prove—was somehow altogether too academic a task.

"The literature of crime has always been a personal interest of mine: I've no doubt my colleagues in the Department of Psychological Medicine could ferret out all sorts of terrible repressions to account for my wishing to wallow in murder and mayhem. All I can offer by way of excuse is the plea that quite a number of people who never commit a violent crime of any sort share this dubious taste. They must do, or how would novelists like Chandler and Simenon, let alone our own school of brilliant detective writers like Agatha Christie and Michael Innes, possess the following they do? What I find especially enthralling is the relationship between the novel of crime and suspense and the so-called serious novel, and I propose to devote a good deal of attention to what might be called borderline cases—*Our Mutual Friend* comes to mind and I expect all of you will be thinking of the entertainments of Graham Greene and that mixed masterpiece, *Crime and Punishment.*"

What a liar I am! he hopelessly acknowledged, for he knew very well that not one of the dutiful, expectant faces now lifted from the new exercise books or unsullied sheets of file paper was likely to have been bent over Dostoievsky; perhaps, he told himself, they would know of the Dickens even if they hadn't read it. You are not here to despise your students, his conscience tartly reminded him: and as for lying, that was a worse one you told a little earlier. What you find especially enthralling at this moment is the presence of Mrs. N. Jones, housewife, who has escaped for a couple of hours from a round of endless pleasure; sipping vodka by her heated swimming pool, planning to spend Christmas on the ski slopes or where the remote Bermudas ride, surely not in Bantwich. The faces turned to him began to show some consternation: he took command of himself, he returned to the lecture room, to his own position on the rostrum, he drank from the glass of water thoughtfully provided. When he looked up again the fair head of Mrs. N. Jones was half hidden behind the coif of wholesome Sister Marie Louise. He turned to the blackboard, found a piece of chalk and wrote the words *"Crime Fiction, Past and Present"* in large letters and a steady hand. Then he turned round and talked sensibly, amusingly and comprehensively on the origins of the Gothic novel. After three quarters of an hour he opened Baird's box of books and began to distribute the copies of *The Mysteries of Udolpho* and *Caleb Williams*. His students lined up and signed for the volumes they selected.

"We keep several copies of each book we mean to study in detail," he explained for the benefit of Mrs. Jones, though the younger nun and a rather fine-looking elderly man were nearer to him and in just as much need of an explanation. "Most of them you could get from a public library or in paperback, but many people find borrowing from our own stock more convenient."

She borrowed, she signed; then left the room, conspicuously on her own in the crowd in the passage, following the sign that pointed the way to the refectory, for the sacred moment had arrived: members of different classes would now mix and mingle, regarding each other with curiosity or suspicion or hope. By the time Mr. Roberts had finished handing out books and locked the box, his class had disappeared up the broad mahogany staircase. Miss Blount, Mrs. Landor, Mrs. Berg awaited him on the mezzanine under an oil painting of roughly pre-Raphaelite vintage depicting Florentine youths and maidens disporting themselves amorously under the dark admonitory gaze of a sort of Dante-figure with a raven perched on his shoulder. This was a work not at all to Mr. Roberts' taste, but no doubt he would learn to like it, he dismally allowed, knowing how the shifting tide of what was currently considered fine or deplorable would sooner or later carry him with it, and even lead him to suppose this portentous bit of humbug exactly as splendid as the devotees of the *Zeitgeist* chose to think it.

"I have just been telling Miss Blount she mustn't read these books at bedtime, Mr. Roberts. She would never get a wink of sleep."

"Miss Blount is tougher than she looks," Mr. Roberts said, and thought that indeed she must be. "I should think she might sup full with horrors any night of the week without any risk to speak of. Now *you*, Mrs. Landor, are a great deal more likely to be upset by skeletons in chains and raving maniacs. I remember how bothered you were by Clarissa's deathbed." Having killed two birds with one stone, supplying each lady with the desired image of herself as strong-minded or throbbingly responsive, he suffered them to buy him with a coin of Mrs. Berg's and much fluttering innuendo, a cup of coffee. This he bore off with a sudden revulsion to a lonely table as far away as possible from the ladies of his class, judging correctly that on the first night of a new session they would have as much or more to say to each other in his absence as under his eyes.

It was not solitude he wanted, and it was not actually Mrs. Jones, or he might have joined her on the spot: she had picked an easy chair in the far corner of the spacious room and taken from a side table a copy of one of the intellectual weeklies provided by the administration. He picked up a journal himself and sat on the corner of the table, just taking in at a gentle angle and from a slight eminence the physical fact of this young woman's presence. He noticed again what had struck him about her earlier in the evening—how a first impression of her astonishing beauty was rapidly displaced by the discovery that she was not after all, particularly beautiful. Her features were pleasant, her colouring, discerned by him to be natural, was lovely; she had moved, she now sat with simple grace. Finding that the final fell far short of the first estimate seemed somehow to do her a subtle and ineffaceable wrong; he was never to see her in the coming weeks without being aware of some vulnerability in her which augmented her effect upon him past any point beauty could have reached without its aid.

She was not to remain alone for long; a shadow fell across her page and across Mr. Roberts' quiet appreciation. She looked up, she smiled so completely that the reflection of her smile crossed his own face—fatuously enough since the smile was for another man, younger than himself, very much better-looking, not however her husband, Mr. Roberts knew, for this man was an old acquaintance of his, and clearly of hers, and his name was not Jones, it was Faraday. Mr. Roberts looked diligently and unseeingly at the *New Statesman*, which might as well have been *Playboy* for all the mental satisfaction he could find in it at such a moment; but feigned absorption could not protect him. He had been seen and recognised.

"Roberts, dear chap, how are you? It's an age since I

saw you—bring your cup over here, tell me what you've been doing these last two years. Nan dear, this is a friend of mine—Roberts, this is Nan Jones."

"We have met. Mrs. Jones is in my class this year."

"Is she really? Nan, you must have changed—why, when I first knew this girl she would no more have read a book than swum the Channel or gone to the moon or acted Lady Macbeth."

"You haven't changed at all," Mrs. Jones said: crisply, rather. "Just the same old demonstrative Nick, anything goes as long as it produces an effect."

Mr. Roberts looked and felt uncomfortable, sensing animus, considering flight, but was immediately and effectively rooted to the spot by Faraday's ever so pleasantly assenting to the girl's proposition by leaning forward and tugging with a none too gentle hand at Mr. Roberts' beard.

"Roberts has changed, he didn't have this when I went to Canada. What hair he had then was on the top of his head."

Nicholas Faraday was in fact rather a pleasant, quite intelligent, fairly able young doctor who had married early, assisted his wife in the rapid production of four children and was now driven to augment his income as a senior registrar in the Bantwich City Hospital by lecturing often to nurses and occasionally, as on this particular evening, to mature students on such topics as "The Problems of Healthy Retirement" and "Is There a Case for Private Medicine?" There was no harm in him, but when Mr. Roberts felt those clean, neat, medical fingers fasten upon his facial hair while that bland young voice made comment on his receding hairline, instincts stirred within that took him back rapidly to his apology a short hour ago to his new class. Somewhere within him was concealed undoubtedly a veritable monster of aggression, a fiend who would for instance, had a knife been conveniently to hand, unthinkingly but with relish have plunged it between the younger man's ribs even in the presence of Mrs. Jones and other witnesses. As he quietly detached himself, as he left Nicholas Faraday and the girl together, he hardly knew which of his two selves he most despised, the primitive animal of lecherous intent and murderous proclivities or that Mr. Roberts beloved of Miss Blount, Mrs. Landor and Mrs. Berg who could walk away from the younger people with a polite word, a smile and an absolute determination to forget the whole episode as fast as possible.

CHAPTER TWO

"And how are you? And why are you here? And does old Steve let you out at night all by yourself? Or is he— don't tell me—baby-sitting?"

Nan's gaze had followed Mr. Roberts across the room, as if she took some responsibility for his flight, indeed as if this flight had made him for the first time clearly visible to her. She kept her eyes on him while she turned Faraday's questions over, selecting the two that had to be answered and leaving the others to take care of themselves.

"Old Steve is dead, Nick, and my mother is baby-sitting."

It was just as well she was not looking at the young man; his flush of embarrassment must have pained her.

"Ah, I didn't know—I've only been back a couple of months, and finding a house and settling the kids at school seems to have taken up most of the time. I haven't seen anyone, I haven't heard any of the local news. What happened? Or don't you want to talk about it?"

She turned round to face him. "I don't care one way or the other. It makes no difference, does it? It's eighteen months old, my bit of news. The winter before last, a car accident, icy roads, a bit of fog just outside Leicester. Seven cars piled up and Steve's was one of the badly damaged ones." There was a very long silence, which

only she could break. "I was pregnant, that helped."
After another silence she added, "My little boy is very
like Stephen to look at."

"Are you, you know, working? How do you manage?"

She shook her head. "I shall work again when Davy's
old enough for school; just for the present I don't think
it's fair to make him do without the only parent he's
got."

"Then you're—" He did not like to say "poor" or
"hard-up," so she kindly said it for him.

"No, I'm not poor: we live with my parents and they
insist on keeping us so that I needn't touch what Steve
left. That way there'll be something for our child later
on."

"And it works? You can manage, the four of you
together?"

"We manage. And it seemed, you know, the best way
at the time."

"I am very sorry, Nan," he said at last. "I would have
written if I'd known."

"I'm sure you would. How did you like Canada?" she
said next, since her widowhood, as a topic, seemed to
have exhausted itself.

"Not much, not at all. No, actually I quite liked it, but
Jill didn't and the kids hated the schools. And we never
meant to stay, two years was just about right."

"And what are you doing now?"

"Anaesthetics at the City Hospital. It's pretty fierce."

"Goodness! Give my love to Sister Harper: she won't
remember me but none of her nurses would ever forget
her."

"She'll remember you. Even behind a mask Nurse
Broadbent was quite an eyeful."

"You do say cheering things." Then she added, "I'm sorry I snapped at you when you came over."

"Yes, why did you?"

"I suppose I didn't like your sort of telling Mr. Roberts I was, you know, not specially keen on books. Actually you made me sound a bit of a moron."

"My dear Nan, I never meant to. I'm very sorry. Though I can't see why you should worry about what impression you make on him. He's quite harmless and very nice and used to, well not morons, but not exactly senior wranglers."

"You're getting in deeper and deeper," she said, not unkindly.

"Yes, I'd better shut up. Anyway I have to get back to my class."

"Is it something interesting?"

"I'm only doing two evenings out of ten, I shouldn't think it would be worth your while making a switch."

"Oh, Nick, you're hopeless!" she said with a laugh he didn't at all understand. "I mean, what's the course *about?*"

"Oh, that: 'The Law, the Doctor, and the Ordinary Citizen.' I'm doing criminal negligence tonight, and some time in November I've got an evening on 'Drinks, Drugs and Driving,' if you're interested."

"No, I don't think so," she said in a strange voice, and as they both stood up, for the refectory was emptying, students were politely holding doors and standing back to let yet older students pass, she added, her voice still different from how he had remembered it, "Stephen was drunk the night he got killed. Actually he was supposed to have caused the accident."

The lecture theatre was full, or as full as twenty-four people and a lecturer could make it, when Mrs. Jones came in. I hope she isn't going to make a habit of delayed entrances, Mr. Roberts thought sourly, feeling premature sympathy with his regulars and the disturbance she might cause, twice on every evening that the class met, holding them up, creating such a flurry and stir. But the flurry and stir was in his own breast, nobody but Mr. Roberts was at all disturbed and she held up nothing, since all that had so far happened was that the faithful had sat down again in their places and started to examine the volumes they had taken from the book box. Conversations about the summer holidays, begun upstairs over chocolate biscuits, continued now in unabashed tones; so that he had finally to rap discreetly on the lecturer's desk and summon their wandering attention. "For the benefit of those of you who haven't previously attended our classes," he began, "we usually spend the second part of the evening discussing some of the points that the more formal talk in the first part may have raised in people's minds. Generally speaking, I try to throw in enough controversial statements to provoke a good argument and give anybody who cares to a chance to express his or her own views and perhaps lead us all to conclusions quite different from the ones I've previously suggested. This sort of improvisation on a fairly restricted theme can be most rewarding in a class of mature people."

Since nobody however seemed inclined to interpret this statement of intent as an invitation actually to speak, Mr. Roberts rapidly revised it, producing a direct challenge.

"Why do you think ordinary law-abiding men and women read books about violent crime?" he asked a man in the front row; but this unfortunate saw the direct question as an attack and shrank further into his collar and tie. "Well, Mrs. Landor, possibly you can help us here. I reminded you a little while ago how upset you were by Clarissa's death—in a novel by Richardson we read last year," he explained for the benefit of the new students, "and yet I clearly remember that you also told us you greatly enjoyed the book. Is it possible, do you think, to enjoy being disturbed and frightened—as long as the characters in a book are going to do the actual suffering?"

"Oh yes!" the ladies assented. Miss Blount was heard to remark in a penetrating tone to her neighbour, that she hadn't quite realised at the time that *Clarissa* was a detective story, and would they be expected to read it again this year, because she had found the small print somewhat trying?

"Yes, because otherwise people wouldn't go to see awful horror films, would they, about vampires and tomb-robbers and things?"

Mr. Roberts seized thankfully upon this slender piece of evidence that someone was with him, and was even prepared to offer verbal testimony.

"Exactly, Miss, Miss—would you mind letting me know your names if I haven't seen you here before? It makes my task very much simpler."

"Turton, Mrs. Turton."

From then on discussion proceeded in a lively and not too disconnected manner. An hour passed, the iniquities of the Labour Government came into view at the end of a long prospect of moral responsibility for crimes against the person, the value of retributive punishment, the role of the environment in shaping the criminal personality; and Mr. Roberts, who had learned painfully over many years that only in the most academic and indeed most sterile of academic circles could any literary discussion be confined to literature, recognised that bounds were in danger of being exceeded, and that a firm lead must now be given.

"Then I think we're agreed, aren't we, that an interest in, even a sort of fascination with criminal acts, especially when these involve some element of physical danger is so widespread as to be easily excused. The more squeamish among us, or the less honest, can't read with any acknowledged pleasure accounts of actual crimes in newspapers, real horrors that have happened to real men, women, or alas, children, without a degree of sympathetic involvement that ruins any chance of vicarious satisfaction. So we turn thankfully to the writings of Dorothy Sayers or Ian Fleming or"—he smiled down at Mrs. Berg, Mrs. Landor and Miss Blount, who was probably asleep—"Dennis Wheatley, where we can attend, so to speak, the gladiatorial combat or the public execution with a clear conscience because it never really happened. And some of the best-loved writers in this genre recognise fully that we don't want, we positively fear, to have our delight sullied by any appreciable concern for victim or suspect. Hence the number of mysteries where the crime has already been committed before the start of the narrative, or where the victim is a wicked person for whom no real sympathy need be felt. We are not usually asked, in the classic detective story, to feel with the characters, to identify, only to perform a feat of the intellect. You open a detective story in the mood in which you might attend a sherry party—you expect enjoyment, interest, amusement, all at the level of your mind that tackles a crossword puzzle. But you approach a serious novel as you go to meet someone you greatly care for; your expectation is pitched higher for delight, but you admit the possibility of disturbance."

Liar, liar, he raged—for when did you, Roberts, last expect any enjoyment at a sherry party; and what meeting à deux is this that you postulate; and when, in your experience, has such a meeting yielded any delight worth the effort of memory? And as if promptly to remind him of that time in his life when such things were possible and even frequent, Barsted, the porter, at that moment opened the door of the lecture room, coughed discreetly, and announced that there was a telephone call for him in the secretary's office.

"I did ask the lady to call again, sir, or to leave a number but she said no, it was urgent. A Mrs. Harvey, she said. I have asked the girl at the switchboard to put the call through to the warden's room."

Mr. Roberts paled. As Barsted reported in due course to the others of the domestic staff, he looked as if he had seen a ghost; and lest this be thought to cast discredit upon the good man's capacity for original and piquant metaphor, it should be said at once that Mr. Roberts had seen exactly that: an apparition, the shade of somebody once almost as well known to him, he had foolishly thought, as his own humdrum solid self, now scarcely to be recognised in the bearer of a name no longer even hated or feared; very nearly, most days of the week, forgotten.

"Thank you, I'll come," he got out, and mustered presence of mind enough to say good night to his ladies, to remind them to pass the register around and tick their names, to say how much he looked forward to seeing them all again next week. A slight, quite unintended emphasis, fell on the word *all* and he caught Mrs. Jones's eye, for she had risen already. She had been among the first to stand up, as if she couldn't wait to get away. A strange and wonderful thing, however, happened; for she responded to his appeal with a brief sweet smile, as if she had noticed the emphasis, taken it to herself and found some pleasure in it. With this scarcely-to-be-breathed-upon impression he took himself off to the warden's room, and through the cool exchanges of the next few minutes weighed that tiny hint of future joy against the ponderous certainty of past pain. His former wife's voice had not changed; heard across more than a hundred miles of English industrial midlands it had the same familiar edge. Even while asking his help its undertone was careless and contemptuous.

"I hope I've interrupted nothing. That man seemed reluctant to bother you."

"I was lecturing, but it was over more or less."

"I tried your home number first. Your mother told me where to find you." A little flick of disdain on the word, mother, put back the clock five years on the spot. To think, she had once cried, that she should be living in a crude sort of music-hall joke—to think any man should ever have asked her, of all people, to show a little consideration for his mother! "She didn't like to tell me, she didn't sound at all pleased to hear my voice."

"What is it you want, Audrey? I take it there must be something wrong for you to get in touch with me."

"Yes, there is. Bill has disappeared." Since he said nothing she added, "He left home just over a week ago to spend a few days in London. He should have been back by the weekend. It isn't the first time he's altered his plans without a word to me, so I took no notice. Then on Sunday night I had a phone call from the manager of the hotel where he was staying. He'd gone out on the Thursday morning leaving all his luggage in his room, without paying his bill. They haven't seen him since."

"I'm sorry," Mr. Roberts said, unable to think of anything else to say, and surprised that he could utter so much without misrepresentation. For he was sorry; he had very much disliked Bill Harvey, for a short time he had even hated him, but lately he had come to see his wife's lover as his own saviour; if he were sorry for no other reason, the thought that Harvey's disappearance might cause this woman to seek him out and disturb his days once more would have been enough. But it was not quite that, for side by side with his more bitter feelings he had had some sense of fellowship with his brilliant rival; had admired Harvey's good brain and bright academic prospects; had seen his contributions to learned reviews and heard his talks on the Third Programme with mingled admiration and envy; had often thought that he had lost Audrey to no ordinary run-of-the-mill adulterer, but to a man who outstripped him in every measurable way. Not that one could exactly boast of the capacities of the fellow who cuckolded you, he ruefully considered, while he repeated his words with a sense of their total inadequacy. "I'm very sorry, Audrey."

"Is that all you can say? Haven't you seen him?" Her tone as much as her words took his breath away.

"Greg? Greg, are you there, Greg?"

"Yes," he said with difficulty. "Why should I have seen him?"

"Because of that damn fool letter you wrote me. Did you know you only put a fourpenny stamp on? I only got it this morning."

"Just a minute. Just a minute, I wrote you no letter. I don't know what you're talking about."

"Oh, isn't it just like you to be so pedantic," she cried, "fussing about words at a time like this. Typed, then, if you must score off me."

"I'm not fussing about words," he said, his sense of reality dwindling moment by moment. "I never wrote or typed or sent you any letter. Will that satisfy you?"

It was her turn to be silent, a state that never endured for long.

"Well, if you didn't, Bill must have. And he must be

in Bantwich, because it's postmarked Bantwich and it
caught the afternoon post on Saturday. Are you sure you
haven't seen him?"

"Oh, don't be a fool, Audrey. If this is some trick
Bill's playing on you, you can't imagine for a moment
I'd join in."

Silence again; then she said, with less assurance, "It
wasn't just the postmark, it was the message or whatever
it was."

"Unsigned?"

"Unsigned. I'd know which of you sent it if it was
signed, wouldn't I?"

"Audrey, for God's sake—an anonymous letter! Don't
you know you should just tear things like that up,
without reading them?"

"I might have, if it hadn't been for Bill's going off,
and the postmark."

"Was it obscene?" he asked, lightly now, for he began
to see daylight; it wasn't beyond the Harvey he remembered to desert a woman after four years of marriage and
then send her a ribald reminder, in circumstances as
embarrassing as he could make them for somebody else,
Roberts for preference.

"No, not obscene."

"Threatening, then?" Not so amusing, he thought,
even by Harvey's standards.

"I can't make head or tail of it," she said, "but no, it
isn't threatening either. It's a couple of lines of poetry. I
don't recognise it but you might, and Bill would have if
he'd been here."

"Wait a minute. Was this letter addressed to Bill or
you?"

"To me, of course. I wouldn't have opened it otherwise."

Wouldn't you just? Mr. Roberts managed not to say,

and then thought that in the circumstances she would surely have been justified. But she was going on. "I'll read it to you, shall I?"

"By all means."

"Ye fields of Cambridge, our dear Cambridge, say, Have ye not seen us walking every day?"

After a moment he said, "No, I don't recognise it: I could make a guess but that's not good enough. I can see why you thought I might have sent it. But I didn't."

"Then you won't mind if I pass it on to the police?"

"The police! Why on earth should they be interested?"

"He's disappeared," she said patiently, as to an idiot child. "I want to know what's happened to him: supposing he's had an accident or lost his memory or something? I thought I'd get in touch with you first, because I wouldn't like you to get into trouble."

Her cool assumptions stupefied him.

"What sort of trouble? Even if I'd sent you two lines of seventeenth-century verse in an envelope, that's hardly a criminal offence. I strongly advise you to go to the police at once and set your mind at rest." He put down the receiver, surprised to find that his hand was shaking so violently that the clumsy movement almost knocked the whole instrument flying, and glad that he was alone, that Barsted the porter had had the tact to have the call transferred to the privacy of Dr. Bentley's room where nobody could hear or see him, and only the faint line of light under the communicating door showed that Prothero was deputising for the warden as he generally did on Tuesdays. Prothero now came through that door wearing a look of patent curiosity.

"Ah, Roberts: I heard somebody in here and wondered what was amiss. The warden was playing bridge

tonight, so I hardly thought he would have honoured us
with a visit. Did you wish to see Dr. Bentley?"

"No, I was on the telephone," and, blast your
curiosity, Mr. Roberts would have liked to add, but did
not. "Barsted had the call put through here."

"A sensible man, with more initiative than people of
that class can generally be counted upon to display,"
Prothero said. "Your students will have dispersed by
now, no doubt. Did you supervise the signing of the
register?"

"No, I didn't." Some of my exasperation must have
got through to him, Mr. Roberts perceived, for he is not
pleased; he is looking round for an excuse to throw the
book at me. "My ladies are conscientious to a fault.
There is no need for anyone to stand over them."

"You know best. But we have to justify every penny
of our expenditure these days and keeping up the
numbers is part of the exercise. A word to the wise: I'm
sure you take my point."

Mr. Roberts took himself off, feeling that his patience
had been strained enough for one evening. His class had
disbanded into the rapidly cooling night air, Mrs. Jones
along with the rest; and though he later looked up and
down the street in the irrational hope of catching a
glimpse of her and allowing that impression to wipe out
some of the disquiet Audrey's telephone call had induced
in him, she was nowhere to be seen.

CHAPTER THREE

"It was very kind of you to make time for me to see you. I expect you're a busy man."

Mr. Roberts looked up from his writing table, suspecting sarcasm; for coming as he did from an understaffed and overworked city police department in an era of increasing crime how could this quietly spoken young detective inspector with the Birmingham accent and the neat moustache concede that a man like himself knew the meaning of the word busy? Inspector Hunt met his gaze blandly however and his tone had been friendly and respectful. Mr. Roberts selected a rather noncommittal reply.

"Friday is one of my easy mornings. How can I help you?"

"Would you have any idea, sir, what brings me here?"

"Mrs. Harvey spoke to me a few nights ago on the telephone."

"May I ask you, sir, exactly what she told you?"

"She said that her husband had vanished from a hotel in London; a day or two later she had received a letter with a Bantwich postmark. For some reason she thought the contents of the letter suggested that I had sent it, though it wasn't signed, no address was given and the thing was typed."

"Exactly so, and very neatly put if I may say so. But

of course an English scholar would be bound to express himself—succinctly, wouldn't you say?"

"They don't all," Mr. Roberts said, rather tartly, with a thought for some of his colleagues.

"And that was all the information Mrs. Harvey passed on to you?"

"All I can remember. Except the actual words of the letter; it was two lines of verse."

"Can you repeat them, sir?"

"Ye fields of Cambridge, our dear Cambridge, say, Have ye not seen us walking every day?"

"Would you say, sir, you have an exceptionally good memory for poetry?"

"A good one. I don't know about exceptional."

"It would be one of the tools of your trade, I dare-say?"

"Perhaps," Mr. Roberts said guardedly, though he could not quite understand his urge to be guarded in the face of the inspector's frankly admiring tone. He was soon enlightened.

"Because Mrs. Harvey tells us you claimed not to know the lines in question, or to have any idea where they came from. But of course the reference to Cambridge might have helped to fix them in your mind. Mrs. Harvey informed our colleagues there that she met Mr. Harvey when you were working in Cambridge and she was an undergraduate."

Mr. Roberts had a question of his own and this seemed the moment to put it.

"Do you think, Inspector, or do your colleagues in Cambridge think, that anything has really happened to Harvey?"

"We wouldn't be at all surprised, sir. That's about as much as I'm prepared to say at the moment."

"But what? I mean at the very worst, what could have

happened? Supposing he'd been—oh, knocked down by a car, or had a heart attack—"

"His wife reported his disappearance forty-eight hours ago, sir. There's been ample time to check on accident victims and hospital admissions."

"Did his wife tell you he was, well, unreliable? He's perfectly capable of running off for a week or two, with a young woman for preference?"

"Mrs. Harvey thinks it unlikely that he did anything of the sort this time. Because you see, sir, he abandoned his luggage at the hotel—a very smart pigskin case, some new clothes of high quality, including a fine dressing grown and some rather special underwear." The inspector's tone evoked a powerful atmosphere of healthy Midland nonconformist disapproval. "The very things that in his wife's opinion he would have taken with him on an escapade of that sort."

"She should know," Mr. Roberts said, and stopped in horror at the intense bitterness of his own tone; the inspector could not have missed it. His expression as he glanced up from his notebook showed sudden keen interest, hidden almost as soon as felt.

"No, there seems no reason to suppose Mr. Harvey didn't intend returning to his hotel on the evening of the day he disappeared. He had booked his room for another night, he had told his wife and at least one of the friends he saw in London that he was returning to Cambridge for the weekend. He'd spent one day at a conference on Tutorial Methods in the Seventies, held at King's College in the Strand: on the following day he recorded a talk for the BBC—"—here the inspector flicked back some pages and consulted his notes—"on Hartley Coleridge, whoever he might be, and then he saw his publisher over lunch and went back to his office with him; he was asked to undertake some work on commission, very important his wife seemed to think it, several volumes with notes and introductory essays, she says he was thrilled about it. And his publisher confirms that. The chap at the BBC too, they're both quite clear that he was full of beans, if you'll pardon the expression. I daresay you could put it in much more literate terms."

I daresay I could, Mr. Roberts thought, such as cock-a-hoop or high as a kite or bragging and swaggering and playing to the gallery as usual, but I won't. Instead he said, "What you are saying, I think, is that nobody believes he was in the sort of state that made them wonder if he might commit suicide."

"Is that what I was saying?" the inspector asked, respectfully or mockingly, Mr. Roberts could not tell which.

"And if he hasn't fallen ill, or been hurt in an accident, or committed suicide, what do you suppose can have happened to him? He's not a wealthy man, nobody would have kidnapped him. And he's a humanist, not a physicist or a mathematician, he'd have no access to any information that could possibly interest a foreign power." Mr. Roberts gave up, his imagination having extended for a dizzy minute to its uttermost limits.

"There are just two other possibilities," the inspector said, "as you'll see if you think about it. Either he's gone away deliberately, which seems unlikely if you remember his luggage, or he's been put away." He waited a moment to let these two suggestions sink in. Then he looked over his shoulder and spoke in another voice. "Is that your typewriter?"

The question came so sharply, so definitely, after the hazy series of conjectures that Mr. Roberts almost jumped out of his chair. He did not, he controlled himself rigorously, he looked across at the familiar old machine on the broad windowsill in as casual a manner as possible.

"Yes, of course."

"You own, or the firm's, so to speak?"

"My own. I use it a good deal."

"Would it be very inconvenient, then, if we were to borrow it for a few days, just to see whether by any chance somebody might have used it to type out some poetry recently?"

"It would be very inconvenient." I am *angry*, Mr. Roberts told himself, I am not frightened, what have I to be frightened of? "I haven't written to Mrs. Harvey in five years," he said angrily. "Why should I lie about it?"

"If you haven't written to Mrs. Harvey in five years, sir, you can obviously have no reason at all to fear that we will be able to identify this machine as the one on which Mrs. Harvey's letter from Bantwich was typed."

"I don't fear anything of the sort. I need my typewriter."

"I daresay you would be able to borrow one for a few days, sir, if the need is pressing. Of course I would prefer to leave you your own, but in that case an unpleasant construction might be put on your reluctance to let our experts examine it."

"Oh, take the bloody thing!" Mr. Roberts shouted: the sound of this man shouting was strong enough to silence the voices of women talking in the next room, so that the quiet that followed his cry had a desperate and expectant quality. Then one of the women giggled, the spell was broken.

"I'm glad you see it my way, Mr. Roberts. I will give you a receipt for it, of course, and I can assure you that you will have it back just as soon as we can be sure that it wasn't the one used by whoever did or didn't use it, if you follow me."

Mr. Roberts could not smile.

"Supposing just for a moment that what I know is impossible were possible: I mean, supposing my machine could have been used by somebody to type the letter to Mrs. Harvey—what happens next?"

"That depends very much, sir, on whether Mr. Harvey turns up, and how he turns up." The inspector waited a moment to let this sink in. "If he's alive and well our investigations will obviously come to a halt. The anonymous letter wasn't obscene or threatening, there would be no question of a prosecution for abuse of the postal services. And at the moment we've no real reason to think that he isn't alive and well, have we?"

"No reason at all," Mr. Roberts said steadily.

"Just as a point of interest, sir, did you look it up?"

"Look what up?" Mr. Roberts said. This is called playing for time, he informed himself severely but with interest.

"The quote, the Cambridge bit. Because I'd have thought that to a man like you trying to find out where it came from would come as naturally as—oh, say, checking alibis, to a man like me. I'd have thought you wouldn't be able to rest until you'd traced it. Unless, of course, you knew it already."

Mr. Roberts licked his lips.

Inspector Hunt got up and looked along the rows of books on the well-filled shelves: one of the joys of the brand-new glass and concrete building of Bantwich University's Faculty of Modern Languages, and the staff thought these joys rather few, was the generous provision of storage space; there was a place for everything except the human beings condemned to work there. Near the window Inspector Hunt found what he wanted, a row of editions of individual poets.

"Could you advise a near-illiterate like me where to look now?"

"Cowley," Mr. Roberts said, as expressionlessly as he was able. "I did look it up," he added.

"Did you now?" the inspector said, with some complacency for his remarkable insight into the workings of a scholar's mind. "How do you set about a job like that?"

"Style," Mr. Roberts said bitterly. "Tone, cadence. It had to be seventeenth century or very early eighteenth. And it's too gentle altogether for the great guns, Marvell or Dryden. So I tried Cowley. I thought I remembered it, as a matter of fact, though I hadn't looked at it for years."

"And you obligingly left a marker in," Inspector Hunt said; his friendliness, which had seemed to wax and wane throughout this interview, reached a high point with Mr. Roberts' revelation of some of the milder technical niceties of his occupation, only to depart with astonishing speed as he opened the book and turned back a page or two to find the title of the poem.

"Is this some sort of crazy joke, then?"

"Somebody might think so, I suppose," Mr. Roberts said.

"'Elegy on the Death of Mr. William Hervey,'" the inspector read aloud. "Or should it be Harvey—like Derby and Berkshire? That's a fine thing to send the wife of a missing man, wouldn't you say?"

Mr. Roberts said nothing at all. The inspector closed the book; his face was stony.

"I will take this as well as the typewriter if I may. They will be returned to you in due course unless it is necessary for us to hold them as evidence in criminal proceedings."

Mr. Roberts had risen but now sat down again: the

room swayed from side to side, the brilliant white rectangle of sky outside the window tilted at a sickening angle. Through giddiness and nausea a vestige of his ordinary good sense told him that he must be calm, that at this moment of all moments in his life it was of the utmost importance that he should not seem to be unstable, prone to dizzy spells or to paranoid ideas. Important, then, to bite back the words that had come instantly to mind in response to Hunt's phrase, criminal proceedings: words of violent repudiation, words that might suggest he saw himself as victim of some ghastly attempt at character assassination, at some deliberate persecutory attempt on his peace of mind by that man who had stolen his wife and almost rocked his reason five years before. He said with admirable self-command quite other words arranged in the form of a simple question.

"When may I expect to hear from you?"

"Very hard to say, sir." The inspector was at the door, he was briskly professional. "We'll get in touch as soon as we have any definite information about your type-writer—or on Mr. Harvey's disappearance, of course. I would very strongly advise you, Mr. Roberts, not to put us to any difficulty in finding you, should we need to do so."

On that none too reassuring note he left. Mr. Roberts stayed in his room, closing his eyes against the glare. You have a brain, he told himself, and this is the time to use it. Since Tuesday evening you have known that somebody, presumably Harvey, is out to make trouble for you, to embarrass and harass, to needle you. Whatever satisfaction he may expect to get out of it you have it in your power to deny him. If you refuse to be rattled, if you carry on as if nothing has happened, if you fix your thoughts on your work, on your students, on that lovely girl who ought, God knows, to act as a distraction to any man this side of senility, you'll be denying the bastard his infantile gratification. And how will he know that? And what evidence of my suffering could he expect to get? Mr. Roberts' good mind was now working with something like its ordinary precision, and he found the answers to these questions easily enough. Harvey is not in Cambridge; he must have been in Bantwich on Saturday when that letter was posted. So he may well still be here, even lurking around the university or the Chambers, which anyone could do without exciting comment, so diverse are our students these days; he may be waiting for evidence of my discomfiture. He may hope to hear of my being borne off to hospital, or jumping in the canal, or taking an overdose, knowing that I have done two of those three things before. If that's what he wants he won't get it. I shall show him that his pranks and poses are a matter of absolute indifference to me; that the past is dead and gone, and I can still at the age of forty envisage a future. In that way I defeat his malice.

"And of course," he said aloud to the blank space on the windowsill where his typewriter had lately stood, "the police will find that I did not type that letter. I have nothing to fear from them."

He almost succeeded in convincing himself: when the machine was returned a few days later with a polite but uninformative note and a neat parcel containing his Cowley arrived at the porter's lodge, his conviction was complete, he put the whole incident behind him. Audrey did not write or phone.

CHAPTER FOUR

By the third of November the weather had turned raw and unpredictable. Nobody at the Chambers was much surprised at the shrinkage of classes; Mr. Roberts watched ten of his quota shuffle in with moderate gratification. There was a smell of sulphur in the air, fog was a distinct possibility, nobody could be blamed for staying by their own fireside. The nuns were there, Mrs. Berg had brought Miss Blount in her car with apologies from Mrs. Landor, she was so dreadfully sorry, such a shame when they were just going to start Wilkie Collins, but her hip had been giving her trouble, the doctor had been adamant, she must stay indoors while the weather was so damp, she sent her love, she would be back just as soon as ever she could. Mr. Roberts smiled reassurance to the nuns and to the pugnacious civil servant, who had shown in the past three weeks a remarkable taste for esoteric horrors and a fair acquaintance with the works of Edgar Allen Poe and E.T.A. Hoffmann. Then he saw that Nan Jones had not seized an excuse for staying away, that she had brought her undemonstrative yet compelling presence once again into this dull room, was for the fourth time to present him with something pleasant for his eye to fall on as he searched the room for a response to a question or asked for points of view. She wore a new coat reaching to her ankles; the colour was a startling

orange but the hem had already been splashed. She took
it off and put it on the back of her chair with a little frown
of annoyance, missing altogether his words of greeting,
quite forgetting to smile in his direction. "Such a pretty
coat—what a shame!" Miss Blount cried over her
shoulder. If the length of her outer garment made it liable
to damage and defilement, the brevity of the dress Nan
now revealed drew a little chorus of gasps from the old
hands: oh, she is so young, Mr. Roberts thought, why
ever does she waste her time on this dingy place, what
can her husband be thinking of? Only Mr. Peachment,
whom the weeks had revealed as a taciturn individual
who had retired recently from a lifetime of dispensing
drugs in a London hospital, followed her in. By seven
forty-five it was clear that no others could be expected.
Mr. Roberts was resourceful in dealing with such
contingencies.

"Since half the class has taken a look at the weather
and decided not to come, we won't start on an important
writer tonight, or next week I should simply have to
cover all the ground again, which would be very hard on
all you brave and virtuous people." Pause for appreciative laughter, Miss Blount disclaiming courage, "Kind
Mrs. Berg simply brought me, or I'm afraid there'd be
one fewer still." Then he went on, "I thought we might
do something rather different—leap ahead to the present
day and consider some of the special difficulties of
today's writer of crime fiction. For there *are* difficulties
that Poe, for instance, never had to take into account
when he was writing *The Murders in the Rue Morgue*.
And they grow, year by year, these difficulties."

"You mean, the police are so much cleverer these
days?" Miss Blount suggested. "I remember a little play
I watched on television, there were great big Alsatian
dogs and a helicopter, and I remember thinking what

little chance the criminal had, and do you know?" she smiled around at her fellows with a shade of anxiety, "I really felt quite sorry for the poor man, although of course he had no business strangling the young woman even if she were what used to be called, I think, of easy virtue."

Ten minutes and several episodes of *Softly, Softly* later Mr. Roberts succeeded in steering the discussion back into something like the direction he had initially meant it to take.

"It wasn't so much improved methods of detection that I had in mind," he explained, "for of course I'm not thinking of the difficulties facing the real-life murderer; what the crime writer must find harder and harder as time goes by is to think of a number of plausible reasons why any human being should ever commit murder."

"Oh, but they do," Sister Marie Louise said unexpectedly. "They do, and generally it is their own husbands and wives and children and parents."

Mr. Roberts tried again.

"Yes, you are perfectly right, and that's just what I mean. In real life murder is often a simple family affair, tempers are lost, a rather brutal man strikes his wife in the presence of his son, his son rushes at him with a bread knife. That's the way it really happens, and it would make a book for Simenon, perhaps, as it would certainly have made a book for Dickens, but not for the sort of writer we generally have in mind when we talk of detective fiction. To start with, that sort of family situation often takes place in overcrowded homes in great cities, and nobody could write about such things without asking us to examine our consciences a little about the society that allows these conditions. And we've agreed, I think, that the essence of the detective story is that it will tease and even frighten us a little but it won't upset or anger us."

"That sort of thing's just sordid," Mrs. Berg said, and the opinion of the class was clearly with her.

"Yes. Now would anyone like to say what he or she thinks is the necessary basis for the type of puzzling crime we enjoy reading about in Agatha Christie or Michael Gilbert, for instance?"

"Decent people," Mrs. Berg said, "with butlers and big country houses, all that sort of thing. Nice people who make wills so it's worthwhile for their heirs to murder them."

"Who's got anything to leave these days?" the civil servant said. "I work in the Inland Revenue," he said with the slightly reckless demeanour of the man who knows himself to be engaged in some such antisocial occupation as running a strip club or publishing underground literature; indeed Mr. Peachment and Mrs. Berg, who sat on either side of him, shrank perceptibly further into their heavy winter clothing. Having revealed so much, he would not balk at still more rash exposure. "I deal with estate duty. People who think they're worth quite a bit, people whose heirs think they've something to look forward to, we cut them down to size. In fact my advice to anyone who thought of doing their old man in for the sake of his worldly goods would be, come and have a chat with me first."

He sat back: a slightly dismayed silence followed. Mr. Roberts came to the rescue, for how could he desert the only other articulate male present in his hour of need?

"Thank you, Mr. Bell, you've put the point admirably. Gain used to be the crime writer's favourite motive. All the possible heirs of a rich man or woman could be made into suspects, and we all so disapprove of everybody's greed except our own that there wouldn't be any danger of a reader identifying uncomfortably with the potential murderer. But now large estates, landed property especially, are so hedged about with tax liabilities that a fortune worth killing for really needs to be in the millionaire class."

"Very nice too," Mrs. Landor was heard to murmur, and there followed a digression on living on capital, credit cards, hire purchase restrictions and the unpopularity of counter-inflationary measures, to which the ladies plentifully and delightfully contributed, while Mr. Bell retreated into the remote silence Mr. Peachment seemed quite unable ever to abandon. At twenty past eight they emerged from a morass of financial half-truths with a measure of agreement on the basic fact. It was clear that Mr. Bell and his colleagues had done the whodunit-reading public a grave disservice.

"While we drink our coffee," Mr. Roberts said, "you might just like to ponder a very sweeping statement I'm about to make. If murder for gain has become less plausible in the last few years, nearly every other motive I can think of offhand has also lost a good deal of its compulsive quality. Think, if you like, of blackmail, of hated marriage partners, of guilty adulterous liaisons and illegitimate children whose existence must be concealed at all costs. Then we'll see, in twenty minutes' time, how much more difficult it is to write a good convincing detective story today than it was in the twenties and thirties when the vicarage tea party sort of tale reached its extraordinary zenith."

The refectory, like the lecture room, was by no means as full as usual. There were several eager amateur Egyptologists attending Professor Hallam's special lecture, with slides, on the cultural patterns of the Upper Delta in the fifth millennium before Christ: there were a few young married women, towards whom Nan Jones looked as if she might gravitate, from a course on the emotional problems of the preschool child; there were some solid-looking citizens who had come to hear Nick Faraday on "Drinks, Drugs and Driving"; the title had also attracted a couple of long-haired young men in clothing quite inadequate for the time of year, so that Miss Blount, as she settled into her favourite chair, remarked to Mrs. Berg that she very much hoped that young man had left his sweater in some other part of the building as he was asking for pneumonia wearing nothing but a—what was it called?—a T-shirt, although it was a very pretty one, what was the design actually, she couldn't quite make it out from where she sat? Mrs. Berg peered forward, gasped and sat back, but Miss Blount had fortunately lost interest, and was assuring Mr. Bell and Mr. Peachment that she personally had never had the slightest difficulty with the Inland Revenue, her dear father's accountant simply filled in all the forms for her; for some years now there had been no forms to fill in, possibly the accountant had, like her dear father, passed on? Should she perhaps attempt to get in touch? And when Mr. Bell assured her that there was no need, the Inspectorate would no doubt have all the relevant information and would write to her should they require any contributions, she said—sharply, for Miss Blount— that that was not in the least what she had in mind, had he no conception of an after-life in which the injustices of our present existence might be remedied? Mr. Roberts rescued him once again, deftly turning Miss Blount's thoughts from spiritual reunion towards the happy Egyptology students reassembling to go downstairs for the second part of their lecture.

"Miss Blount's father was a noted local collector of antiquities," he told Mr. Bell in passing; Miss Blount, who was perhaps a little upset by the inclement weather, made a positively uncharitable remark about Professor Hallam, who had disagreed with Dr. Blount not infrequently and often publicly over the attribution of various artefacts of the Nile civilisation, on several occasions expressing the opinion that one of the doctor's most cherished personal finds, now happily in the city museum, was, not to put too fine a point on it, a fake. Polite disbelief followed all round. "A fake!" Miss Blount reiterated, nodding quite sternly at poor Mr. Bell, whom she now seemed to associate with the affront to family pride. "Hallam was wrong, of course, he was proved wrong by several experts of considerably greater standing. Professor Hallam, I should say," she said, with an evident return to her usual kind self, "although I never think of him with that title. My father took him on several trips when he was just a student, to me he is still Mr. Hallam, or young Arthur."

Mr. Roberts recalled a recent glimpse of young Arthur, who was now not merely Professor but Professor Emeritus, held several honorary degrees and had retired in Mr. Roberts' own undergraduate days: could Miss Blount ever have nursed a *tendresse* for the young reprobate who cast cruel doubts upon her father's adequacy as a judge of scarabs or whatever the object had been? Was there a sad little story here of divided loyalties and young love early blighted? His gaze took in the lads in decorated shirts and denim jeans; they would never believe that this old lady and that eminent man in the main lecture theatre were once capable of love: they would hardly even credit that a man of my moderate years could have felt urgent sexual passion: can still feel it, he told himself, with a glance across the room at Nan Jones. But she was not alone, or he might have joined her, he was so pleased that she had dared cold and damp and the threat of fog to come to his class, to give him a precious evening of her company. She was talking to Nick Faraday, or rather he was talking to her; and with a shock of revulsion Roberts realised from the sudden turning away of their two heads as they met his glance that he was the subject of their conversation. You have ideas of reference, he told himself severely, why do you think they should waste time and words on you? And with the clinical term, at once so precise and so damning, the nightmare events of four weeks before were chillingly present to him; he recalled Audrey's voice on the telephone, his interview with Inspector Hunt, the absence of his typewriter, the disappearance of Bill Harvey, of whom he had heard nothing more. Because he did not want to waste another moment's thought upon the Harveys he did a thing he would have believed impossible the minute before. He picked up his coffee cup and walked deliberately over to Dr. Faraday and Mrs. Jones, saying quite coolly, "May I join you?" and registering in their shared blush confirmation of his guess. "You were talking about me," he said, "and it must have been something very scandalous and awful for you both to be so embarrassed."

"I was only," Dr. Faraday began, and "Nick was just—" Nan Jones started eagerly, and then they both began to laugh and their laughter was so candid that it could hurt nobody; it was infectious, and in a moment Mr. Roberts was laughing too.

"Nan was telling me how marvellously kind and tactful you are with your dear old ladies—she said going to your lectures was like watching a man trying to steer a stagecoach with a mixed team of seaside donkeys and retired draught horses. And then we just happened to catch sight of you spending your precious break being nice to Miss Blount and wondered if you're buying

yourself credit in heaven or making sure you're not
resurrected as a scorpion."

Mr. Roberts had never looked at his behaviour in this
light; he could think of nothing to say. In any case that
girl's proximity, the lovely soapy freshness of her young
neck, drove all coherent thoughts out of his head.

"Of course," Faraday said kindly, "you've had lots of
practice in handling old ladies, haven't you? How is your
mother keeping? I take it you're still living with her?"

"She's very well, she's remarkable for her age. Yes,
we live together. She won't hear of giving up her house
and I don't like the idea of leaving her alone."

He knew what he sounded like: devoted middle-aged
son of demanding possessive old woman. It isn't like that
at all, he longed to be able to say; it is only a matter of
what is convenient and sensible, especially for a man
who has tried something different and made a pitiable
hash of it. Nan Jones was looking at him with something
of that compassionate respect he thought probably
coloured his own expression when he talked to Miss
Blount, and he was so bewildered by the hurt this look
inflicted upon him that he got up with a strange smile and
hurried back to his old ladies, to outspoken Mr. Bell and
uncommunicative Mr. Peachment.

"Poor devil, he can't have much of a life," Faraday
now asserted, and since Nan looked as if she would like
to know more, told her his own version of Mr. Roberts'
life story. "He's an only son, you'll have guessed that,
completely mother-bound. Quite bright, too, he got a
research fellowship somewhere or other, Trinity, Cambridge I think, or it may have been King's: she actually
let him go, though his father had died quite recently.
Then he married, he didn't tell his mum about it until
they came back from the honeymoon, he knew she'd
hate the girl. And, by golly, she did. He brought the poor

young woman back here when he was a junior lecturer and she had to live with the old lady—neither of them had a penny, his mother saw to that. Anyway it didn't last long, she ran off with one of his brilliant friends from Cambridge."

"How do you know all this?"

"I was houseman at the Royal when he tried to do himself in: made a rotten job of it, too, not enough tablets and Mum got his note too soon, he'd been in such a hurry to post it he hadn't realised it would come before he was anything like done for."

"Nick, I thought doctors weren't supposed to tell people about their patients?"

He had the grace to look somewhat ashamed but decided to put a bold face on it. "You aren't people, you're a friend."

"He's very nice, I think, quiet and unassuming."

"Just so long as you only think of him as a dear old fuddy-duddy teacher; because it all adds up, you know, to a decidedly odd personality. There are lots of things I haven't told you, I've been very discreet actually, all sorts of fascinating material emerged when the psychiatrists took him over."

"He's not very old," Nan said, in a decidedly cool tone. "About thirty-seven or eight, I should think, give or take a few years. Supposing," she said, getting up and taking her handbag off the table where their coffee cups had been abandoned, "I were thinking of him as a dear young teacher?"

"Well, you can't say I didn't warn you," he said with irrepressible good humour. "Doctors can break professional confidence when they honestly believe it's for the public good."

"I won't report you to the BMA or whatever it is."

"The GMC actually."

"But I hope you don't tell anyone else what you've just told me. Anybody can choose an unsatisfactory marriage partner, it isn't a crime. I did it myself."

She left him to his discomfiture, which did not last long. Mr. Roberts had already left the refectory.

"Now," he began with an attempt at briskness when the class had reassembled. "We've thought a little about gain as a motive for murder, and agreed that it must be rather more difficult for a writer to make it plausible these days. But that's nothing to the difficulties he would be likely to encounter if he started looking around for a real mixture of motives, in order to provide for a classical selection of five or six suspects. What about jealousy, for instance. Have any of you anything to say about that?"

Nobody had; looking at the blank expectant faces, Mr. Roberts thought, I could tell them something about jealousy, and how corrosive it is, how almost anything seems possible and nothing is too bad; in a book one could still make one man kill another because he made a pass at his wife—but in life one simply starts thinking about divorce. Or I did, and God knows I was jealous enough. He saw that the silence had lasted too long, expectancy was giving way to perturbation.

"Divorce is easier now, society generally accepts that marriages do break down and that perhaps nobody should be blamed too much for that; certainly nobody's prospects in his career, for instance, would be likely to suffer nowadays because he was known to have committed adultery or been the guilty party or the co-respondent on a divorce suit. So all those stories where a lover has to kill a husband who won't give up his wife don't ring true any longer; and the idea of a man murdering his wife's lover"—he kept his voice steady with an effort nobody remarked, except possibly Nan Jones, who dropped her eyes rather than meet his at this point—"has a distinctly period flavour in the 1970s. Unless of course one postulated mental illness; insane jealousy does provide a motive and it turns up in tale after tale, but it isn't easy to make credible an insane character who doesn't stick out a mile from any group of likely suspects."

"Everybody does not take divorce so lightly," Sister Marie Louise remarked, and the young and pretty nun nodded her head in agreement with such conviction that Mr. Roberts found himself wondering if concealed passion for a married man had led to her taking the veil; he recalled how only a little earlier he had been imputing to Miss Blount a disappointment in love, and saw that these two romantic explanations of simple events could both be traced to his own preoccupation. He was glad of a moment's respite when Sister Marie Louise went on in her gruff voice, "If one party in a marriage were a Roman Catholic and the other were not, there would be ample motive there for an unscrupulous third party."

Since the nuns generally said nothing at all, Mr. Roberts beamed approval. "Motives for all three parties, wouldn't you say?"

"A practicing Catholic would not be likely to consider homicide a less heinous act than the civil dissolution of the bond of Holy Matrimony," Sister Marie Louise said in a shocked tone.

"No, no, of course not," Mr. Roberts hastened to admit, "but please don't forget we're talking about books, not about life. I only want to suggest that a skilled writer could use that situation and no doubt work out some interesting casuistries among the protagonists." He was in deep water, the mention of the word casuistry had increased the good nun's unease and clearly perplexed

some other members of the class. "Blackmail," Mr.
Roberts said at once, to avoid possible breakers ahead.
"What about blackmail as a motive? Countless good
stories have begun with a person or persons unknown
murdering a cold-hearted blackmailer. How plausible is
that nowadays, would you think?"

"People don't have so many guilty secrets now," Mrs.
Jones said. "It's all part of what you were saying a few
minutes ago. Nobody would really lose their job or be
hounded out of society because they were having an
affair, even a homosexual one in the last year or two.
And nobody would kill anybody else for knowing they'd
been a member of the Communist party or the British
Union of Fascists. And if you have ex-concentration
camp commandants you'd get in difficulties with things
like foreign accents sticking out a mile; all right for a
thriller, but not for a whodunit. I suppose if one had
served a long prison sentence and one's employers didn't
know about it, somebody might threaten to tell; or if one
had taken part in a big bank raid and there was a witness
and they thought they'd get more by blackmail than by
going to the police and claiming a reward."

"Good for you, Mrs. Jones!" Mr. Roberts cried, with
what some of the older members of his class thought
quite an unnecessary display of appreciation. She went
quiet red in response to his praise and their sideways
looks of slightly patronising approval; this was the first
time she had contributed to the discussion, and it will
certainly be the last, Mr. Roberts thought, if I don't
moderate my rapture and take everybody's attention off
her, and how am I to do that when I so rejoice in hearing
her speak, and speak to the point? "Yes, I am sure we
must all agree," he resolutely told the class, "that past
criminal activities known to one person only would still
provide a very real motive; I doubt whether any

convincing whodunit-type book could be written now without something of the sort being brought in. What about continuing criminal activities; supposing somebody were known to be a pedlar of drugs—might a blackmailer, for instance, insist on a share of the profits?"

"I should think that sort of thing does go on, goes on all the time," Mr. Bell said. "But criminals probably think of paying out that sort of money the way honest people think of their income tax—nasty but inevitable. Most people don't actually try to do their tax collectors in, they've sense enough to know there's plenty more where he came from."

"Yes, indeed," Mr. Roberts said gratefully, for Mrs. Berg and the rest had taken their eyes from Mrs. Jones.

"That's sordid, too," Mrs. Landor said. "Not Mr. Bell's line of work, of course," she added with heavy irony, "the drug pusher, the criminal classes. You don't get that sort of person in good hotels or on luxury cruises."

"I rather think that's exactly where you do get them," Mr. Roberts said, "because when Mr. Bell's done with the rest of us we haven't money enough for the *dolce vita*. Yes, I think we could certainly give credence to a crime set in—where shall we say—in a millionaire financier's yacht off the coast of Madeira; gain and blackmail and protection rackets and perhaps even some unnamed vice, if there are any left, will all pass muster in a setting like that. But none of them, alas, will do for a country parsonage or a solicitor's office or a weekend golf club or a school or a hospital or any of those odd places detective writers often write about with such enjoyment. For that sort of background, motives have had to become more and more esoteric—"

"There's a great deal too much of that sort of thing

going on everywhere nowadays," Mrs. Berg said sharply, and her gaze fell unmistakably on Nan Jones's knees.

"Have any of you read a very brilliant early book by
Michael Innes?" Mr. Roberts cried in desperation. "I
can't recall the name, it's some years since I've read it
myself but it's a perfect example of the kind of preposter-
ous notion I have in mind. An enormously wealthy
fellow buys up various freaks; he's making a sort of private collection of psychological anomalies, a kind of
Chamber of Horrors after Freud and Janet rather than
Madame Tussaud. Finally he decides to provide a rather
fancy castle he's collected, with an authentic phan-
tom—"

"The Daffodil Affair," Mr. Peachment said, or rather
mumbled, and then, as the eyes of the class turned in
surprise at this useful reminder from their resident
Trappist, as Mrs. Landor had christened him in a
moment of fun, the sound of people in the hall outside,
people flocking past from the main lecture theatre where
Professor Hallam had evidently exhausted his subject,
forced him to repeat this title, quite loudly, twice over,
until he was almost ludicrously shouting at the class. In
several years of classes given in this very room Mr.
Roberts could not recall hearing an answer bellowed
over such a hubbub; and now above the general
maddening din there came a horrifying extra sound, a
long drawn-out scream, a succession of eldritch yells,
noises surely hysterical. I can call spirits from the vasty
deep, Mr. Roberts thought, for these extraordinary cries
indeed belonged to the museum of phantasmagoric
curiosities he had been postulating only a moment
before. Then the stout mahogany doors of his own
lecture room were opened, and one of the porters, with a
chalk-white face, called through the gap, "Will you
come, please, Mr. Roberts? Will you tell the ladies and

gentlemen to stay where they are for a moment? Mr.
Baird asks if you can join him at once, as the senior
lecturer on the premises." And lowering his voice he
added in what events were to reveal as a fine line in
understatement, "There's been an accident, sir, Professor
Hallam is not himself."

CHAPTER FIVE

Barsted, the porter, in the way of his kind, was a very big man, something over six feet tall and well proportioned. He cleared a way through the front hall and the short passage leading to the main lecture theatre with an ease Mr. Roberts, who was only of average height and girth and less than average assurance, could never have managed. He had seen these places of more or less public access crowded before, when famous men had lectured or celebrities had been secured for a recital, but the mood of the people thronging around him now was one he had never encountered in his life, possibly because he had never attended a prizefight or been present at a really deplorable road accident. Actually the majority of those who had been attending Hallam's lecture were only anxious to get away as soon as possible, but a small minority was speculating noisily on what it had just seen, or thought it might have seen, or believed somebody sitting near the front of the hall to have seen. The woman who had screamed was seated now at the bottom of the stairs having some of that cloudy reviving fluid that appears as by heavenly dispensation in any situation where fainting might occur pressed on her by a waitress from the refectory. Under Mr. Roberts' uncomprehending eye as the porter steered him past she dashed the glass to the ground with an even

louder shriek than she had produced half a minute earlier.
"If you think"—she now sobbed to attendant spirits—
"I'd set my lips to anything to eat or drink in this place
now—" but somebody had thought of Dr. Faraday
upstairs and voices assured the poor sufferer that a real
doctor was on his way, she should just put her head
between her knees, there now.

Mr. Roberts never knew whether she thought this
order safe to obey for by this time he was in the theatre
and Barsted had closed the door behind them. "Don't let
anyone in," he now admonished the junior porter who
had opened the doors to admit them, "not till Dr.
Faraday comes, that's Mr. Baird's orders."

The lecture theatre was a handsome room, semicircu-
lar in shape, with raked seats round the curved side. A
platform occupied most of the straight wall, with steps
leading up on either side. Curtains of a bold geometrical
design covered the windows on this wall which over-
looked a grimy paved yard and two outlying wings at the
back of the building. There was a grand piano on the
platform, pushed to the back at one side, while a
speaker's dais with chair and table stood on the other. A
white screen was suspended in front of the curtains, and
on the table there were some pieces of pottery, a tiny
carved figure of Annubis and a crude wooden doll, and
in odd contrast with these ancient objects a modern
carafe of water and a glass. In the chair sat or slumped
the late Professor Emeritus of Egyptology in the University of Bantwich, and there could be no doubt that he was
dead, nobody could be that extraordinary colour and still
live. Humphrey Baird, who was also a different shade
from his usual glow of health, but lightly green rather
than duskily purple, stood by the chair.

"What happened?"

"He finished his lecture. He invited people to come up

and look at these things he'd brought along. He seemed just as usual. Then he took a drink from the glass here and—well, I can't describe what happened next. Nobody had actually got on to the platform, people were hesitating, you know how they do, putting their hats and coats on, not quite sure if they should take up the great man's time—so some of them got a good view of what happened. One woman became hysterical. I can't blame her, I felt like screaming myself."

Mr. Roberts could understand that. "Couldn't we cover him up, do you think? There isn't anything any one can do for him, surely?"

"Nick Faraday's coming down. Rob, I sent for you because Prothero's skipped off, Barsted said he left ages ago, and Dr. Bentley's never here on a Tuesday, so you and I are the only seniors around, and I thought you'd be likely to keep your head in an emergency."

This, Mr. Roberts supposed, was a kind of compliment.

"Is there an emergency? I mean, you've sent for a doctor. There doesn't seem to be anything else to do."

Then he remembered the woman on the stairs, thrusting the glass of sal volatile away from her.

"My God! You surely don't think he was poisoned?"

"It looks terribly like it, Rob. Of course it may have been coincidence, he might have had a heart attack or a stroke, but from where I was sitting it looked as if he just swallowed whatever there was in the glass and—sort of choked."

"I see. You realise all the people who were at his lecture are getting out of the building as fast as they can?"

"I don't see how we can stop them, do you? I mean we don't *know* that Hallam hasn't just died in an ordinary way; I don't even know if we ought to get on to the police until Nick's had a look at him."

Dr. Faraday came in neatly on his cue: well, he at least doesn't go green when he sees something nasty, Roberts thought sourly, and I wonder what colour I am?

"Sorry I took so long. There was some idiot woman howling on the stairs. What's happened then, old boy popped off in public, eh? Apoplexy, by the look of it."

His tone, which Mr. Roberts found offensively flippant, was oddly at variance with his deft purposive movement, lifting the professor's eyelids, feeling at his wrist.

"His radial artery's like a cord. I should think he's had arteriosclerosis for years. Well, he's certainly given his audience value for money."

"That's what it was, you think, Nick—arteriosclerosis, a stroke?"

"Oh yes, I should think so; but of course that's only a quick guess. We'd better get in touch with his own doctor. What about next of kin? Is there a Mrs. Hallam?"

"There was," Mr. Roberts said. "He's been a widower for a long time. There's a son in the south somewhere, I believe. We could get Miss Angus to telephone his home number. He may have a housekeeper or somebody who can tell us where to get in touch with him."

"You don't think," Baird said hesitantly, "we ought to get on to the police?"

"The police—why on earth?" It was plain that the idea had never entered Faraday's head.

Baird looked helplessly at Mr. Roberts, and for an extraordinary moment Roberts had the impression that he was weighing up very rapidly the chances of anyone else mentioning to Faraday, or indeed to somebody outside the building, his incredible impression that Hallam might have taken poison. The moment could not be prolonged; there was not, Baird seemed to realise, the faintest chance that so powerful an intimation of evil intent could be concealed or forgotten.

"He took a drink out of that glass just before it happened—the stroke or whatever it was. It's all non-sense, of course, but I couldn't help wondering if the water wasn't water, if you see what I mean."

Again he gave Roberts that look of helpless appeal; why appeal to *me*, Roberts thought irritably, I can't help him.

"Not water?" Faraday said in a tone of frank disbelief. "Smell it, Roberts, will you?"

Roberts picked up the glass and sniffed gingerly at the rim before Baird could stop him with an anguished hand laid on his sleeve.

"I'm sure we shouldn't touch—Roberts, your finger-prints!"

"Fingerprints?" Roberts said stupidly.

"Oh, don't be absurd," Nick Faraday said. "You heard me tell him to pick it up. I take full responsibility if there's any to take. You've gone off your chump, Humphrey, if you really think some loony's tried to murder a harmless old boy like Hallam under the noses of eighty or a hundred people."

Roberts still held the glass, held it tightly in fact, though he had almost let it slip from his fingers on Baird's admonition. His own nose was wrinkled, he stared at the others without quite seeing them.

"What is it, Roberts, what's wrong?"

"The smell. It isn't water." He held the glass out to Baird, to Faraday. "I think it's cyanide," he said. Then he began to tremble, and set the glass down only just in time.

"We shall have to send for the police now," Baird said to Faraday, quite calmly now that his worst fears seemed to be confirmed and any hope of avoiding publicity, scandal, the nastiest kind of gossip was as dead as the poor slumped figure in the chair: he went over to the porter, who had spent the last ten minutes stolidly rearranging the late lecturer's slides in the box that held them while keeping a not too obviously interested eye on the doings of his superiors. Words passed: Barsted nodded and left them.

"He'll see the building's cleared. So many people have gone already there can't be any point in trying to hang on to the rest. Except the fainting lady. She must have seen what I did. I should think the police would want to see her."

"I'd better ring my wife. Might be here for hours, if I know anything about the city cops. Anyone you ought to let know, Roberts?"

"Need I stay, do you think?"

"Don't want to worry Mum, eh?" the unspeakable Faraday suggested. "She probably won't believe you, not if she knows you've been chatting up a pretty young widow. Tell you what, I'll ring her, shall I? I'll say you've been held up here, and not to wait up for you, how's that?"

Roberts said, "I could ring her myself if there's any need. But I can't imagine the police will want me here; I wasn't at the lecture, I didn't see Hallam die." All the while an inner voice shouted at him, pretty young widow, pretty young widow, can she be, can this clown be right about that, could he really know?

"They'll want your fingerprints," the clown pointed out. "Because there may be others on that glass besides yours and Hallam's. I really think you'd better hang about a bit, old man."

Barsted came back.

"The police are on their way, sir, and the screaming

lady is ensconced in the ladies' rest room, and I have asked one of the waitresses to bring down a tray from the refectory. And Miss Blount is at the door, she wishes to come in, and she is most insistent. She claims to be an old friend of the professor's."

Over what felt like an enormous chasm of time Mr. Roberts recalled that moment, earlier in the evening, when Miss Blount's evocation of young Arthur Hallam had for a little while opened the door on her own lost girlhood; for the first time since he had followed the porter here, he saw Hallam's body for what it really was, the mortal remains of a man who had lived some eighty years, had been in turn child, boy, hopeful young student, brilliant researcher, internationally know authority, husband, father, widower, and now was so much dead flesh, remembered words, a name on the spines of several books; "Yes, let her come in," he said to the porter in a tone of quiet authority; and since Baird seemed a little taken aback by his intervention, since Faraday looked somewhat amazed that his permission had not been asked, he said with full determination, "Miss Blount knew Hallam when she was a girl; she has a perfect right to take leave of her friend."

The porter ushered her in; there was nothing dignified in her shuffling gait; her garb was the usual mixture of fur and feather she thought appropriate to the winter months. She came down the steps, Mr. Roberts went halfway up the steps to meet her, to warn her that she might be distressed by the dead man's appearance, to make sure that she would at least suffer no agonising shock. "What a one he is for the old ladies!" Faraday remarked loudly: the two walked together to the dais.

"Poor Arthur," Miss Blount remarked in a surprisingly dispassionate voice. "But he has not been the same since Charity died."

For a moment Mr. Roberts and Baird supposed that she was making some general remark on the lines of *Change and decay in all around I see*. She did not allow them to entertain this view for long.

"Charity made him a good wife in many ways," she said now, "and the Snettisloe money was very useful to a young scholar, particularly at a time when grants were not so generous as they are now and travelling fellowships rather rare. He could hardly have travelled so widely," she explained to the three men and to the porter who still stood by the projector, "on any little money I might have brought him. But who knows, there might have been compensation in our domestic life. I believe my temper was more equable than Charity's, though of course I had not her artistic gifts any more than her fortune. All these charming paintings, you know"—she waved a vague hand round the lecture theatre where no paintings of any sort were to be seen—"were her work. She was considered most talented for an amateur. I believe they were a devoted couple." Her voice shook for the first time. Mr. Roberts and Humphrey Baird did not look at each other. Then she said, her tone quite strong again and now with a carrying note of disapproval. "She died first, she died a long time ago. I would not have left him alone. As you see, I have survived him." She turned to Mr. Roberts. "Would you be good enough to help me up the steps? Mrs. Berg is waiting to drive me home."

He did as he was asked: he was at the doors of the lecture theatre delivering her to her friend when the police arrived, in the person of Inspector Hunt and another man in plain clothes. For a moment the inspector seemed not to recognise him; then his eyes narrowed, and Mr. Roberts, whose thoughts had been full of Miss Blount and before that of mortality and earlier still of the debt he owed the clumsy thoughtless Nick Faraday for his revelation of Nan Jones's husbandless state, now lurched back over four more or less ordinary weeks to his ex-wife's telephone call and Bill Harvey's disappearance, to a scrap of Cowley's poetry and a sense of sinister purposes in which he was somehow involved. Then he realised that he owed something else to Nick Faraday, the presence of his fingerprints on the glass out of which Professor Hallam had perhaps drunk poison. It was just then that Barsted, holding up to the light the last of Hallam's slides, exclaimed aloud. All their eyes turned to him.

"This wasn't in the box at seven o'clock this evening," he said. "I went through them all with the professor. There were statues and tombs and some of that fancy writing, hieroglyphics he called them, but I never saw this one, and it doesn't look like it's got anything to do with Egypt."

Humphrey Baird made a movement as if to take it from him, but Inspector Hunt intervened in a voice of quiet authority, much like that Mr. Roberts had used earlier to secure Miss Blount's admission. "Show us what it is please, and handle it as little as possible."

Barsted moved the slide holder, and pressed the switch of the projector lamp. Since the theatre lights had not been turned down the picture showed up in poor contrast on the screen, and for a moment nobody could quite make it out.

"Whatever's that, then?" the inspector said in evident frustration.

"It's an eagle," Humphrey Baird said. "Just a moment, I'll switch the lights off."

The picture became plain. A bird of prey—not an eagle, perhaps a falcon—held in its claws the curved agonised body of a rabbit whose blank gaze, already dulled, made more intense the bird's rapt glare.

"And what does that mean?" Inspector Hunt said.

"Just a mistake, I should think," Baird said. "A slide from another lecture slipped in with this lot."

"I went through them with the Prof at seven o'clock," Barsted said. "I told you. It wasn't here then. You all right, sir?" His tone became solicitous: Baird had turned on the lights to reveal Mr. Roberts sitting on the edge of the dais with his head in his hands.

"Probably been a bit too much for him, all this excitement," Nick Faraday said, gently for him. "Very nasty goings-on, first that"—he indicated Hallam's body with a wave of the hand—"and now this." He extended the gesture to include the picture on the screen. "Nature red in tooth and claw, that's the first thing that came to my mind when I saw that miserable bunny rabbit. That's a quotation from something or other," he said kindly to Inspector Hunt. "Mr. Baird here could place it for you, I daresay. Poetry's not much in my line."

Humphrey opened his mouth, but Inspector Hunt silenced him with a peremptory movement.

"Or Mr. Roberts? Mr. Roberts is a dab hand at contexts, isn't he?"

Mr. Roberts raised a pale face and essayed a smile.

"Oh, that's an easy one, Inspector. Any schoolboy doing English A Level would get it right. It's from Tennyson's 'In Memoriam.'"

"I see. And what's 'In Memoriam'? I did some A Levels myself," Inspector Hunt said with heavy irony, "but not English, I'm afraid. Physics and Chemistry and History, that's what I thought a policeman would find useful, not knowing a fancy murder like this would be coming my way."

"It's an elegy," Baird said, with a concerned glance

for Mr. Roberts. "Tennyson wrote it for a friend of his called—oh, God! called Arthur Hallam."

An hour later, when statements had been taken and a police surgeon had arrived, Mr. Roberts was dismissed. Nan Jones got up from the bench in the hall where she had been sitting with her long vivid coat wrapped warmly round her cold legs.

"Mrs. Jones! It's very late." The words were idiotic, he realised as soon as he got them out. He found some others, no more intelligent. "Were you waiting for me?" And when she nodded, he thought how little faith he had in Dr. Faraday and said so softly he could hardly hear himself, "Why should you do that? Won't your husband be worried?"

"I can't tell you here—why I waited, I mean. I haven't a husband, he's dead, and I have telephoned my mother, she knows I'll be late."

He stood there in a daze. Incidents in his former life had tended to space themselves out. So slow had he been to realise his wife's infidelity, so slow were the processes of law when he invoked them, that the sharpest drama of his days had dragged itself out over months, over more than a year, and had lost something of its sharpness in that weary length. Now in a few weeks, a few hours, a few unbelievable moments, things quite undreamed of, a disappearance, a violent death, possible new pangs of involvement, even perhaps love, everything that he would lately have declared impossible in his well-ordered and colourless world had come to pass. The effect was simply for the moment to make him quite incapable of useful movement: the girl put out her hand and took his, very much as he had taken Miss Blount's not long before.

"Have you a car? Is it outside? I'll have missed the

last bus, I think. Would you drive me home, if it isn't too far out of your way?"

The idea of something that needed to be done broke the spell; an extraordinary delight breathed in his voice, poor dead Hallam, poor bereaved Miss Blount, tactless Faraday, worried Baird, the just perceptibly hostile Inspector Hunt were all forgotten. He took his coat off one of the hooks in the hall; he felt in his pocket for his ignition key. His fingers closed on something else, something he had not felt in years, but it was years since he had worn this coat; he had taken it out of his wardrobe this morning on his mother's reminder that he would be late back and the first frost of winter was promised along with the first fog. The little bottle he now held dated from the bad time after Audrey left him, the months of sedatives and tranquillisers, carefully chosen so that his attempted suicide might never be repeated. It was a long while now since he had needed any pharmacist's sugar-coated or encapsulated comforters to see him through the day or ensure him a night's rest: all the same he wished he had not been reminded quite so forcibly at just that moment of the suffering that love for a woman could bring in its train. He found the key and took Nan's hand. He liked the feeling of their hands clasped together, for she is not Audrey, he thought, defiantly informing the fates that he did not intend to be served the same trick twice. "My car's round at the back," he said, and they left the building together, under the porter's faintly disapproving eye. "Good night, Barsted."

"Good night, Mr. Roberts. Shall we be seeing you next week, sir?"

"I expect so. I can't think why not."

"If you say so, sir."

"What did he mean?" Nan Jones said. They were out

on the street, and she spoke with some urgency. "Why shouldn't you be here next week?"

"Barsted has a vivid imagination. I believe he's quite disappointed that the police haven't thrown a cordon round the building and arrested half a dozen of us for murder."

"For murder? Then it's true—Professor Hallam's dead?"

"Yes, it's true. He was probably poisoned. All very nasty, and not at all the sort of thing anyone expects to happen in the Extra-mural Department. But since it has happened, Barsted would like all the trimmings—criminals breaking down and confessing, or making a run for it, preferably with gunfire. It isn't a bit like that. Everyone was very quiet and reasonable."

"Murder," she said slowly, "and on one of your nights, too." And when the significance of this seemed to be lost on him she said, just the least bit impatiently, "It's almost too good to be true, isn't it, you talking away about motives and things, and somebody actually committing a murder at that very time in that very building."

They had stopped on the pavement by his car. Their eyes met.

"Yes, it's odd. And it isn't good exactly. From my point of view it's rather awful. Other things have happened, you see, that you don't know about."

"Something has happened," she said, "that you don't know about."

They were beneath a lamp post and cold blue light was shed over their heads and shoulders. They both looked ill. She opened her handbag and drew out a slip of paper.

"I went to the loo; then I found I'd left my copy of *The Moonstone* in the lecture room, so I went back. Everyone had gone, but this was lying on your desk. Perhaps I should have left it there." Since he showed no urgent wish to take it from her, she added reassuringly, "It isn't obscene or anything, it's poetry, I think."

"I'm sure it is," he said drily. "Tennyson, at a guess."

"I wouldn't know. Don't you want to read it?"

He read it.

"Yes, that's entirely appropriate."

" *'So word by word and line by line, The dead man touched me from the past.'* What does it mean?"

"It's a sort of ghastly joke. Or perhaps worse."

She shivered. "It's fearfully cold. Can we get in your car?"

"I'm sorry," he said with compunction; then added scrupulously, "I think I ought to warn you that I do know what Barsted meant. He thinks I probably killed Professor Hallam."

"Then he's a fool," said Nan Jones.

CHAPTER SIX

It was not Barsted, it was an older, slighter, less military figure of a man, with the less equivocal name of Wilson, who unlocked the doors of the Chambers to Inspector Hunt at nine o'clock the following morning and closed them again behind him. Catching the inspector's look of surprise he explained, "Dr. Bentley's instructions, sir. Everything is to be exactly as usual today. We are not open to the public until ten-thirty on weekday mornings. Reporters were to be kept out, he said, until he had spoken to you. Mr. Prothero is with him now, if you would kindly step this way."

The inspector kindly stepped that way; which was across the entrance hall and to the left, past the doors of the main lecture theatre, now firmly shut and with a hastily written notice forbidding unauthorised entry prominently displayed on one of the central panels. Wilson opened a different door and made an announcement, and the inspector found himself alone with a very large old man, evidently asleep behind a suitably vast leather-topped writing table. Wilson had mentioned two names, the owner of the second now came in quickly through another door; a brisk, indeed bristling man of about fifty, starting to go bald but not yet even beginning to promise the impressive breadth and polish of the warden's great naked cranium, and unlikely ever to show on those small fierce features anything like the other man's apparent benignity.

"Good morning, Inspector. Dr. Bentley, Inspector Hunt is here."

A ripple transitorily disturbed the warden's monumental calm. Mr. Prothero said a little louder, "Inspector Hunt is here, Warden. You wished to see him the moment he arrived."

Dr. Bentley's eyes opened, closed, opened again and expanded to take in the deputy warden and his visitor.

"Have I the pleasure—Prothero, would you very kindly introduce me to this gentleman?"

Hunt was a busy man, and the morning could not be allowed to slip away in vague civilities.

"I am Inspector Hunt of the Bantwich City Police Criminal Investigation Department. I am here to continue my enquiries into the death of Professor Arthur Hallam. Your porter told me that you wanted a word with me before you speak to the press."

"It has all been a very nasty shock."

"Yes, I am sure it has. Was there anything you particularly wanted to ask?"

"A very great shock," Dr. Bentley repeated with some severity. "An institution of this kind—a little temple of self-improvement, a backwater of scholarly interest, so far kept edifyingly remote from vulgar scrutiny—is not lightly to be exposed to the gawps and stares of a populace always eager to decry the intellectual."

Inspector Hunt waited, just managing not to look at his watch. He had heard variations of this speech quite a few times in the course of his professional career. Whether it was a golf club whose secretary had run off with the subscriptions, a bank unlucky enough to hold the account of a customer whose cheques wildly exceeded his credit or his expectations, a firm whose books had been fiddled once too often, every institution or organisation that came under his gaze would sooner or later, generally sooner, throw up a spokesman to beg for, or—as seemed more likely in Dr. Bentley's case—to insist upon, absolute discretion, inviolate secrecy. Though how they imagined he could buy the watchdogs off, he failed to understand, not guessing that the plea was made in most cases, certainly in this case, as a sort of pious offering to the gods. Nobody, least of all an intelligent man like Bentley, a competent organiser like Prothero, could possibly believe that news of Hallam's death and of its attendant circumstances could have failed already to have leaked out: but even the competent and intelligent are allowed to sacrifice on the altar of hope. Dr. Bentley rumbled gently on; from time to time Prothero put in a pointed word of explanation or approval. Eventually, as Hunt had known they must, the words ran out, the voices quavered or ground to a stop.

"I strongly advise you," he then said, "to be as helpful and polite to reporters as you possibly can. Answer specific questions truthfully or refuse to answer them as tactfully as you can. Don't beat around the bush; don't stand on your dignity. After a few days the whole thing will die down. Hallam wasn't royalty or an entertainer or a little girl, he wasn't found dead in a male brothel in his underwear. There's very little here for the vultures to get their claws into." Intercepting frosty looks he added in a more conciliatory manner, "Believe me, even the lads from the local papers will stop bothering you after the inquest—until we make an arrest, that is."

"An arrest!" Dr. Bentley and Prothero chanted in unison, as if such a possibility had never occurred to them.

"Perhaps I should have said, if we make an arrest. This promises to be a fairly complicated sort of case."

"We understood," Dr. Bentley said, and paused as if to let the deputy warden have his say.

"Naturally we assumed—" Mr. Prothero began, and, seeing that he would have to go on, started, as was his habit, to bluster a little, "—I even went so far as to inform the warden that Professor Hallam had committed suicide. A tactless and surprisingly exhibitionistic gesture, I called it. But to my mind this extraordinary tale of the extra slide with the Tennyson reference is undoubted confirmation that the man was entertaining delusions of grandeur."

"He was a somewhat flamboyant character," Dr. Bentley supplied. "He was a little inclined to court publicity. I think we may say that there was a decided element of the theatrical in his makeup."

"You are suggesting that gulping down a glass of cyanide in front of nearly a hundred people was the sort of thing old friends of this man would have expected him to do?"

"Put that way," Dr. Bentley said, with the caution of a very large animal negotiating a very narrow path in the forest, "it certainly sounds extremely unlikely."

"Murder in an Extra-mural Department is even less likely," Prothero said. "That would mean postulating a maniac of some sort."

"It strikes you as a mad thing to do, murdering an eminent man in this public manner?"

"Emphatically," Prothero said, and gave the word itself emphasis, with repeated nods; seeking the warden's eye, at the same time, as if it mattered that his opinion on this point should be reinforced by Dr. Bentley's. But the warden seemed to have wandered off on another train of thought.

"Might we ask what facts your investigations have so far brought to light? I do not know if it is, er, *done* to ask a policeman questions of that kind, I do not understand the etiquette for such an occasion; they are fortunately rare, in my experience indeed unique. So you must forgive me if what I ask is untimely and inappropriate, but it occurs to me that if we are to offer you any help some adequate information about the circumstances of Professor Hallam's demise would hardly come amiss."

"We know very little," Hunt said at once. "We know that he drank from a glass containing hydrocyanic acid, and that the carafe of water on his desk also contained traces of that substance, which is extremely volatile."

"Perhaps you would explain that term? Neither Mr. Prothero nor myself can claim any knowledge of chemistry."

"Hydrogen cyanide, otherwise known as hydrocyanic acid, rapidly turns into a gas in ordinary conditions of temperature and pressure, if it is kept in an open vessel. If Professor Hallam had poured out a drink at the beginning of the lecture and left the glass and the carafe uncovered until the lecture ended two and a quarter hours later, there is a chance that as much of the chemical as would have been left in solution would have done him no harm. However a member of your staff, a Mr. Baird—" Inspector Hunt took out a notebook and flicked over the pages.

"Humphrey Baird, yes, our librarian. You may have the most complete confidence in his testimony, Inspector, he is a thoroughly reliable person, a man of the utmost integrity."

Hunt managed to control the upward quirky movement of an eyebrow at this lavish encomium and went on, "Your Mr. Baird was present from the beginning of the lecture to the end and he is positive that it was not until Professor Hallam had closed the discussion, and invited interested members of the audience to come up and inspect his specimens more closely, that he took the glass off the top of the carafe for the first time, poured out some of the contents and drank. He is also absolutely sure"—here Hunt looked meaningfully at Prothero— "that that was all he did. In other words Mr. Baird has stated with absolute certainty that Professor Hallam did not swallow a tablet or capsule, or empty the content of a phial or an ampoule into the glass of water he poured himself. There is another witness, a lady who was sitting in the front row, who saw the whole process clearly, and although at the time she gave way to hysteria," Hunt paused for a moment, rather pleased by this scholarly turn of phrase, "her account is substantially exactly the same as Mr. Baird's. Both of them are emphatic that the professor's movements and expression, as he got his drink ready, were quite unremarkable. It doesn't seem likely that a man could put cyanide into a drink more than two hours before he intended to take it and not show by some hesitation or oddity of behaviour that he knew he wasn't simply going to quench his thirst."

He paused to let this sink in, but was not disposed to let the pause go for nothing, using the moments when Dr. Bentley and Mr. Prothero stared at each other in something like dismay to glance around the room, as if enlightenment might lurk in its massive bookshelves or the giant painting over the fireplace: four feet by seven of meticulously painted young women—some way after Botticelli—discernibly celebrating the birth of spring with garlands of untimely roses, and hair of a reddish tint braided into extravagant complexities above low foreheads and greyish-green cheeks and lips. Hunt was no connoisseur but an exhibition of paintings by his namesake Holman Hunt had recently toured the provinces and enlivened the Bantwich scene for three weeks; a vague proprietary interest steered him into the art gallery with his wife and children, on a wet Sunday afternoon when he was off duty, and his interest had been sufficiently aroused for him to get up from his chair now and scrutinise the picture closely. He turned to find Prothero's fierce little eyes upon him, with an expression in them he could not quite make out, though certainly astonishment was part of it.

"You are interested in painting?" the deputy warden said, in a slightly annoying tone of incredulity.

"Some. Is that pre-Raphaelite?"

"I fear not," Dr. Bentley said. "If you look in the bottom left-hand corner you will probably find the initials C.S. They stand for Charity Snettisloe, youngest daughter of the Snettisloe who bequeathed this house and Snettisloe Grange to the University of Bantwich. It was unfortunately a condition of the bequest that we should provide a permanent showcase for the lady's rather deplorable artistic efforts."

"They aren't as bad as all that," Prothero put in. "The poor lady hadn't an original idea in her head, and she was about fifty years too late for the pre-Raphaelite vogue, but purely on their technical merits they represent quite an achievement."

"Prothero speaks as something of an expert," Dr. Bentley said, with an appearance of generosity. "He is a gifted amateur painter himself."

"Only in water colours. This sort of thing is quite outside my range."

"We are keeping the inspector from his work," Dr. Bentley now suggested. "And I believe he was just about to tell us how the unpleasant substance that poisoned Professor Hallam got into his drinking water."

"I can't quite manage that yet. But we are reasonably

sure when it got in. Your senior porter, Barsted, brought the carafe, filled in his presence with water from the kitchen tap, down from the kitchen on the first floor next to the refectory soon after he came on duty at four o'clock yesterday afternoon. The doors of the lecture theatre were left unlocked from then until just after seven when Professor Hallam arrived, discussed the slides with Barsted and gave him directions for showing them, and then arranged his specimens on the table on the platform. He asked Barsted to keep the doors of the theatre locked while we went upstairs to have a light meal with Mr. Prothero—you would confirm that, sir?" He looked at Prothero, who nodded. "Barsted locked the doors at about ten past seven and went up to get himself a cup of tea. At seven-thirty he came down, unlocked the doors and stayed near the platform until Professor Hallam himself came in, Barsted is sure of that. And during the interval before the slides were shown Barsted stayed where he was."

"So that if we are to believe that somebody did in fact deliberately poison Arthur Hallam, that person must have been in this building between four and seven o'clock yesterday afternoon?"

"In or around. There is the unlikely chance that somebody might have climbed in at a window; Barsted showed me last night that all the catches were in fact applied, but there is a small door to the yard at the back of the building which is generally locked and bolted. The lock is of a simple pattern and a key could easily be found to turn it. The bolts were drawn during the afternoon and evening. Barsted tells me that he always bolts that door, along with other doors upstairs leading to the fire escape, before he leaves the building at eleven. Could you confirm that that would be his normal practice?"

Dr. Bentley looked at Prothero with a certain intensity of appeal; Hunt discerned a fleeting resemblance between this hairless and oddly dependent scholar and a babe in arms; Prothero's brisk fussiness of manner would have done credit to a busy nanny well used to the exigencies of coping with such a vulnerable infant's daily needs.

"Yes, that's quite usual. The door to the yard is indeed kept unlocked as well as unbolted while the public is in the building—it serves as an additional exit in case of fire."

"So our hypothetical murderer would have had three hours, more or less, to poison the drinking water if he were operating from inside the building, plus about an extra half an hour between seven-ten and seven-thirty-five—Barsted's not positive to the minute when he got down from the refectory—if he came into the lecture theatre from the backyard. What about access to the yard itself?"

"From the fire escape to the upper floors," Prothero said promptly, "and there is a gate on to Back Sparks Lane; but that would certainly have been bolted. It is never used."

It was on the tip of Hunt's tongue to point out that escape from a burning building into a closed yard surrounded by a high wall—and from Dr. Bentley's window he could see how high a wall it was—would be something of an exercise in dangerous and possibly deadly frustration, should such an emergency ever arise; but he held his peace, mentally noting that one of his constables would have to confirm the state of that outer wall and its bolts and assess the chances of anyone scaling the wall.

"Three hours," Dr. Bentley now said: ponderous reflection seemed a strange activity for a babe in arms, but that was what was undoubtedly going on beneath that palpably innocent scalp, as rosy as the garlands of Miss Snettisloe's vernal young ladies, and far more so than their sadly chlorotic complexions. "Does that mean you will be asking members of my staff for an account of their movements over all that really rather long period?"

"Some members only," Hunt said. "If you or Mr. Prothero could suggest to me any that I should particularly make a point of seeing, I would be very grateful."

"I would not like to estimate," the warden said, "how many persons enter and leave this building between the hours of four and seven on a Tuesday evening. A number of them are giving or attending recognised classes, some are borrowing or returning books from and to our excellent library, others merely browsing along the shelves. Some persons, possibly with defects of the senses of smell and taste, actually choose to consume an evening meal in our refectory, which is open to all registered students whether they have a class that evening or not. And for a public lecture, such as Professor Hallam's, a further unidentified and largely unidentifiable group of persons would have access to the building. All these are in addition to our own permanent administrative, academic, secretarial and domestic staff who number about thirty, including myself and Prothero here and Mr. Baird and his assistant Miss Carr."

"And Mr. Roberts?" Hunt said.

"Roberts?" Dr. Bentley said, with a quick lift of the eyebrows, and one of those oddly helpless sideways peeps at Prothero, which appeared to constitute a recurrent demand for support along the thorny pathway of everyday affairs.

"Mr. Roberts is not a member of our staff at all," Prothero said at once. "He is a lecturer in the Department of English at the university. For some years now he has given courses for us. He is one of the numerous men and women we call upon to cope with specialised subjects, so that we may offer a wider variety of courses than our small regular establishment makes at all feasible."

"Does Dr. Faraday come into that category too?"

"Oh yes, indeed," Dr. Bentley said, clearly recalling the brash young doctor far more readily than an unimpressive middle-aged English scholar. "He is employed at one of the city's teaching hospitals, I really forget which. Like many medical men he is uxorious and polyphiloprogenitive and consequently very glad to augment his income in any, er, respectable way. He has contributed here and there to various courses; last night it was most fortunate for us all that he was on the premises just when he could be most helpful."

The warden smiled seraphically, rather as if some extraordinary foresight on his part had led to this happy state of affairs: then he recalled that the state of affairs had been far from happy, and that neither Dr. Faraday nor any of his professional colleagues could in fact have helped Professor Hallam once he had half-drained his glass. His smile faded; his eyes fled back to Prothero.

"You were asking about Roberts," the deputy warden now said. "Is there any special reason why you should be interested in his presence here last night?"

"I am keeping an open mind. At this stage"—if Hunt required to be evasive, he certainly did not wish to appear vague—"observations have to be made piecemeal. It looked to me as if your Mr. Roberts was labouring under something of a strain when we took his statement."

He watched intently: Warden and deputy warden were eyeing each other now, and of the two this time it was the older man who seemed more ready to take the next step, to assume his correct position as head of the household. Prothero looked positively relieved when Dr. Bentley came out with what was all too evidently going through his own mind.

"Roberts is a thoroughly sound and reliable scholar, an excellent teacher for mature students, patient, sensible, never overbearing or pedantic. He is, professionally speaking, a man we all respect and like."

Prothero nodded automatically.

"But—"

Prothero's head changed the direction of its motion, and moved from side to side suggesting a note of warning and regret.

"But, although we discourage gossip in the Chambers and endeavour to close our eyes entirely to the personal affairs of our associate staff, which are of course, no business of ours"—Dr. Bentley paused to allow this to sink in, before delicately revealing the extent to which his own eyes had been opened on the personal affairs of Mr. Roberts—"it is inevitable that, um, major disturbances should come to our notice. And it is common knowledge, I am sure Prothero would agree?"—Prothero's head changed direction once more—"that this poor fellow Roberts attempted suicide some years ago after a domestic crisis of a distressing sort, and was an inmate of an appropriate, um, institution for some months thereafter."

"That would have been when his wife left him?" Hunt suggested.

"Oh, please, please, there is no need for us to go into details: I for one have never felt it necessary or right to probe into such saddening circumstances. Indeed I am not sure whether I have ever been officially informed of the existence of the lady you mention. At social occasions, for instance the Christmas sherry party, I do not recall ever having been introduced to a Mrs. Roberts; we do not pry, we do not wish to take an impertinent interest in what does not in any way concern us."

"I've always made a point," Prothero put in, "of trying to put the poor chap at ease on these occasions by associating myself with him as a couple of crusty old bachelors; that always seemed to me the most tactful line to take."

"Very laudable, I'm sure," Hunt said, with a notable effort to cover his own exasperation. "What it all adds up to, then, is that at least one person in this building last night is possibly a nut case."

The effect of this calculated vulgarity was a sharp intake of breath on Dr. Bentley's part, and the abrupt cessation of Prothero's nodding and shaking, abandoned in favour of an angry stare.

"Nothing of the sort!" the deputy warden said, or rather snorted; and really his pink skin and small dark eyes did give him the look of the pigsty. "All that the warden has told you is ancient history. Roberts is no more a *nut case* than I myself; or you, for that matter, my good sir."

"You haven't noticed, then," Hunt said in his even tone, "his obsession with elegies?"

"Elegies?" Dr. Bentley said, sitting forward in his chair with an expression of fullest perplexity.

"He doesn't, as a regular thing, incline to lecture on funeral odes and dirges, you wouldn't say? His taste in literature doesn't run to the lurid and macabre?"

Dr. Bentley and Mervyn Prothero once again sought support from each other without words; then Dr. Bentley cleared his throat.

"You will know, of course, that he is lecturing on 'Crime Fiction, Past and Present' to our students this session."

"Was that his own idea?"

"I believe it was," the warden said, looking strangely unhappy."

"I'm afraid I must agree," said the deputy warden.

"His real interest," Dr. Bentley said, "is in minor novelists of the late eighteenth and early nineteenth centuries: a fruitful field, you will agree, for the patient worker not particularly desirous of making a name for himself."

Inspector Hunt digested this carefully. "People like Defoe and Fielding?" he offered, from some reservoir of carefully stored youthful browsing.

"Oh, no, no, no, not the greater writers of the period; there is little left to be said about figures of that magnitude, though outstanding critics turning their attention to any period can still find fresh treasure where lesser mortals might suppose the tomb to have been, hum, thoroughly robbed, to use an unsavoury metaphor. One thinks of Trilling on Keats or Dr. Leavis on Marvell and Pope. But Mr. Roberts would hardly consider himself in that category. He has written adequately on some lesser known works of Thomas Love Peacock; he has made interesting contributions on Godwin and that extraordinary woman Mary Wollstonecraft. And he incorporated in his opening lectures this term on some fascinating material on the widespread dissemination on horrific romances, translated from the German, in the circulating libraries of Jane Austen's time."

The warden sat back, believing himself to have rendered Mr. Roberts a service in thus enumerating his modest scholarly achievements to this by no means unintelligent young policeman. If Inspector Hunt had derived any reassurance as to the lecturer's stability or sanity it could not long have survived Prothero's next remark.

"He and young Harvey—Dr. William Harvey, that is, of Trinity—published jointly a paper on *The Strange Luxury of Artificial Fear*—a quotation from a book called *The Mysterious Pregnancy* by one Joseph Fox, I believe." The deputy warden paused to let this sink in. "Roberts himself was younger then, and the paper was widely regarded as a *jeu d'ésprit*, though it was soundly based on well-edited texts of the time. A certain fascination with the darker side of human destiny and behaviour does seem to reveal itself when one looks back upon his career."

"Dr. William Harvey—" Inspector Hunt said, and was careful to let no unusual degree of interest sound in his voice or shape his carefully selected words. "Would that be the Cambridge gentleman who lectured recently on Hartley Coleridge on the Third Programme?"

Dr. Bentley and Mervyn Prothero both nodded this time; examiners at a viva voce examination might indicate the same sort of approval when a shy and inarticulate candidate suddenly produced an inspired answer to a fairly searching question. In the light of their joint satisfaction Hunt allowed himself to expand.

"I take it he's a doctor of letters or philosophy, not medicine—like you, sir?"

"That is correct." The warden smiled and beamed; his manner indicated a pass, perhaps even a lower second.

"Has this Dr. Harvey visited Bantwich recently, would you know?"

"I have no reason to think that he has ever been in this city," the warden said. "Prothero, would you think otherwise?"

"No, Warden. I listened to his talk on Coleridge, and was impressed as usual by his forcefulness and ease of presentation. He has been spoken of, I believe, as one of those whose performance has failed to measure up to their early promise."

"A not uncommon fate," the warden said, and Mervyn Prothero and Inspector Hunt agreed in a muted chorus of subliminal sad sounds that such a fate was not, alas, uncommon.

"A disappointed man?" Hunt suggested. "A chap with a chip on his shoulder? One who might behave— maliciously, shall we say?"

Academic ranks were immediately and unmistakably closed: a blank front of disapproval at this tasteless suggestion was turned to Hunt's slightly mischievous look of enquiry.

"Not in the least."

"Not at all."

"A poet *manqué*—but hardly *maudit*," Dr. Bentley said.

"That's very good, Warden. *Manqué*, not *maudit*. Very fine indeed!"

"What's it mean?" Hunt said, as coarsely as he knew how, for he could not tell how much of this was deliberate obfuscation and what merely a vague scholastic habit of play.

"He once showed considerable promise as an original writer," Prothero said, with a haughty stare.

"Of satirical verse," the warden said. "A mid-twentieth century Byron, he was called by some critics, a trifle prematurely as it turned out. He has published no poetry for many years."

"I see. But to be a failed poet wouldn't incline to make a man bitter in your view?"

"Is this to the point, Inspector?" Prothero now asked, for the warden looked impatient, even cross, and his assistant knew that it did his sixty-year-old digestion no good at all for its owner to be perplexed and annoyed within an hour or two of his simple luncheon.

"No, sir. It probably isn't. Just a little thought of my own."

"If you are so interested in Harvey, talk to Roberts about him," Prothero suggested. "He must have known the man well at the time when they were active collaborators."

"And later, when Harvey stole his wife," Hunt said, and obtained a fleeting but delicious satisfaction from the scandalised pair of faces turned upon him.

"How distasteful," the warden said at once. "I cannot believe there is any need for all this—muckraking or whatever it is popularly called."

"Not the slightest," Prothero said. "Nobody in the smallest degree professionally connected with this institution could possibly be conceived to have committed any criminal act."

"Naturally not," the inspector said, with heavy sarcasm, "so you will have no objection whatever, I am sure, sir, to telling me about your own movements last night between the hours of four and seven. I don't need to explain the relevance of that information."

Prothero opened and shut his mouth quickly; the warden had taken Hunt's question properly enough to himself.

"I have not the slightest objection," Dr. Bentley said, with almost indecent satisfaction. "I made none." And, in response to Hunt's slightly puzzled look, "No movements, or none worth speaking of. I find the early hours of the morning most conducive to, hum, sustained academic work. I rise at five and have completed a considerable amount of my personal reading and writing before breakfast. Consequently I not infrequently sleep during the afternoon and early evening. I had a committee meeting yesterday at 2 P.M. Directly it was over I drove home, put my car away, and went to bed. My housekeeper woke me at seven-thirty when I bathed and dined before going out to play bridge with friends. She will confirm my, hum, alibi."

He looks as pleased as Punch, Hunt thought as he wrote down the salient details and the warden's home address and telephone number.

"And Mr. Prothero will no doubt be able to account for himself just as fully?"

But the deputy warden shook his head.

"Between four and half-past I was in the refectory upstairs drinking afternoon tea with Mr. Powers of the History Department."

"A good fellow, Powers," Dr. Bentley said with an odd effect of smugness. It occurred to Hunt that the good warden was actually somewhat pleased that Mervyn Prothero seemed rather less well equipped to deal with questioning than he himself had been.

"From then until just before seven I was alone in my room working on business connected with the financial administration of the Extra-mural Department." He sighed. "We are passing through a very difficult phase at the moment."

"The inspector cannot be particularly interested in our current difficulties, Prothero."

Prothero looked, Hunt noticed, no less than murderous under this benign reproof.

"Miss Angus, my assistant, and Mr. Baird, whom you have already met, both dropped in during that period. Otherwise I was quite alone."

"Yes, sir, thank you. And at seven?"

"I met Professor Hallam as he came into the building and showed him into the lecture theatre, purely as a matter of courtesy, of course, he has been familiar with this building for far longer than I have. Then I took him upstairs for a light meal before the lecture. He ate very little, he told me he had lunched later than usual."

"And did anything of unexpected interest come out in your talk over the meal?"

Prothero hesitated fractionally. "Nothing at all. I mentioned that I would not be able to attend the lecture myself as I had a prior engagement. He expressed regret. We talked about student unrest and the relatively easy time my colleagues and I have of it, dealing as we do with mature men and women. That was all, as far as I can remember."

"And your prior engagement?"

"A cinema, I fear." Prothero met the warden's decidedly cool look with as cool a look of his own; his next statement was made in a tone of frank defiance. "*Women in Love* was showing. I thought it well done, so far as any cinema representation of a considerable and complex book can be judged on its own merits."

"I enjoyed it myself," Hunt said with careful gravity. "Thank you for your assistance, gentlemen."

"Should we have mentioned, do you think," Prothero asked as the door closed behind him, with a contraction of the features that might be supposed to accompany some slight discomfort of the spirit, "that the late Charity Snettisloe was the wife of the murdered man?"

"God bless my soul, Prothero, why should that be of any interest to the inspector? He will surely discover it when Hallam's next of kin is interviewed. And I cannot see how the identity of the man's wife could affect the issue in any important way. Well, I had supposed, Prothero, that my capacity for surprise had been exhausted by the events of the last twelve hours, and now you have succeeded in surprising me again. Why should that poor dead lady be in your thoughts at such a time—except of course that we must all rejoice she knows nothing of her husband's fate? Perhaps her painting is on your mind?"

"Oh no, no, I had forgotten all about the painting," Prothero said, but did not look the warden in the eye.

CHAPTER SEVEN

It was on the same day that Mr. Roberts, returning to his room in the English Department after a gruelling seminar on Defoe and the Rise of English Journalism, found Nan Jones seated at his desk. For two hours he had needed to keep his wits about him while the brightest of his students kept up a crossfire of question and answer, both infinitely more to the point and infinitely less endearing than the discursive chatter of his Extra-mural classes; and all that time he had longed for the privacy of his own room and the chance to think over all that had happened the night before, to achieve some sort of reasoned perspective; yet at the sight of his visitor his heart both lurched and tightened, his mouth fell open, he became aware that he must look even less like a man confident of his power to charm than usual.

"I hope you don't mind. I've been here ages. I got fed up standing about outside so I came in and sat down."

"Nobody asked you what you were doing?" Mr. Roberts said with some urgency.

"No. I might have been invisible."

"And what would you have said if somebody else had dropped in to see me?"

She stared.

"Just that I was waiting for you, I suppose. Do you mind?"

"No, of course I don't. Indeed I don't. I'm tremendously glad you came. Because, don't you see, if you could walk into this place without anyone taking any notice, looking as you do, somebody else, especially a not very striking-looking man could have come in and used my typewriter."

He had explained this to her the night before, in the twenty minutes they had sat in his car outside her parents' house. He knew now that she was a mother herself, that there was no rich and brilliant young husband to envy, that she was even, though this he hardly yet dared to believe, disposed to think kindly of him. Picking his way through this tangle of assorted notions he lighted on one that required clarification.

"Your little boy—have you left him somewhere?"

"Yes," she said, amused. "My mother's free this morning, she's looking after him. They love a day together, and it's better if I'm out of the way. Otherwise he plays his two doting women off against each other."

At her front gate he had seen a brass plate. Her parents were both doctors, partners in a prospering general practice; the house had been Nan's grandfather's, bought when the suburb was the latest and the most luxurious development Bantwich had to offer its successful professional men. "I didn't want to read medicine myself," Nan had told him, "but now I wish I had in a way; it's one of the few jobs where a woman can earn enough to support herself and a child as well as any man could. My mother could have done that if she'd had to. But I wanted to marry early, I didn't see any point in working years and years and then dropping it all to marry and have a family. More fool me, I suppose." Her tone of discouragement touched him, he had wondered for a moment if it would be impertinent to pat her hand. And now here she was, sitting at his desk, in a different coat made of some softish leather with neat boots up to her smooth knees, and he said as if the words were forced out of him, "I can't believe anybody would have noticed Bill Harvey if they didn't notice you—"

"I had an idea," she said. "That's why I came really. Part of why, anyhow. I wasn't thinking of being a test case, though I'm glad if that's been any help. But I thought if you'd kept that bit of Tennyson we could perhaps do what the police did—you know, compare the type with your machine."

"I kept it," he said, "but I never thought of doing anything with it; it isn't fair that you should be clever as well as beautiful."

She shook her head.

"I'm not beautiful, not really. And I'm not at all clever, please don't expect me to be able to keep up with you in any sort of brainy way, because I honestly couldn't. But I thought, after you went away last night, that perhaps it isn't so awfully difficult to match type. Anyway we could tell at once, couldn't we, if it were absolutely different?"

He had already put the machine on the desk and lifted off the lid.

"Type the same words," she said, getting up quickly to make room for him.

He typed the two lines that only Harvey, he believed, would have been wicked enough to taunt him with. She read them over his shoulder.

"‘*So word by word and line by line, The dead man touched me from the past.*’"

"Here's the other," Roberts said, taking it from his pocketbook where it had stayed all night. That it had been sent direct to him somehow did not make it more venomous than Audrey's message, passed on to him by her and by the police; he handled it without distaste, with feelings that he recognised as healthier, with resentment, with a determination not to be driven into foolish behaviour by a man he could almost imagine capable of murder. For if Hallam had been murdered, and Harvey was concerned to rattle and madden an innocent suspect, that must mean—mustn't it?—that only Harvey himself could have put cyanide in Hallam's drink; and to carry trickery to the length of destroying a life must surely mean that Harvey was insane. He recalled the lantern slide—the perfect visual equivalent of other words in the great poem besides Faraday's *Nature red in tooth and claw,* for nature in *In Memoriam* was also, according to Tennyson, *so careless of the single life.* It was not beyond the man Roberts remembered to arrogate to himself the casual cruelty of a natural force. "He wasn't actually much of a poet," Roberts now found himself saying. "Harvey, I mean. People made a bit of a fuss of him when his first book came out, but it didn't last. He was facile, I suppose. Read aloud, his verses usually had a sneer in them. And that tone doesn't wear well, it isn't something people take to furnish their own minds."

"What about Tennyson, then?" Nan said. "How does he wear?"

"Not too badly, all things considered."

She sighed.

"I'm not educated, you know. I can take temperatures and give intramusculars and make lovely beds for post-ops, but I don't know anything about the things you'd think important."

"My dear," Mr. Roberts said with great daring, "why should you think you need to know things when just by being alive here and now you do us all such a favour?"

A few minutes later they looked down at what he had typed, and at the slip of paper he had brought from the Chambers.

"It certainly looks very much like it," she said at last, in a small voice.

"Yes, it does. The e's and a's are all choked up."

"That's nothing," she said quickly. "Another machine could need cleaning as much as yours does."

"And it's a very common model—the commonest portable of all, I should think."

"Would the police have let you have it back if it really *was* the one?"

"I think they'd have had to," Mr. Roberts said, "because no offence had been committed then; Inspector Hunt made that clear. They let me have my book back too, but I suppose they'll have photographed it. And they would have done tests on the typewriter—the sort of ink on the ribbon, the different pressure I put on the letters, depending which finger I'd used."

"Would that show?" she said eagerly.

"I should think it might."

"Then that would prove you didn't type the message your wife—I mean Mrs. Harvey, was sent."

But he shook his head regretfully.

"I don't suppose Bill Harvey has taken a professional course in typing, certainly he hadn't when I knew him. If he used two fingers like me he'd probably bang the keys in the same way."

She picked up the two samples and looked at them closely.

"They're horribly alike—" She stopped. "What shall I call you? Mr. Roberts sounds silly now, after last night and everything."

"Rob," he suggested. "Not my Christian name, I loathe it. I was Rob at school and when I was a student. Audrey used my first name, especially after things began to go wrong. I'd hate to tell you what my mother calls me."

"I'm Nanky Poo at home," she said, in a matter-of-fact way. "I'll bet yours isn't any worse than that."

They kissed; kissing would not come easily to either of them for some time yet, but at least a start had been made.

"I still don't understand why the wretched machine wasn't impounded."

"Perhaps he's turned up," she said, "gone home. Then there wouldn't be any point in their keeping it, even if it was the one. You said so yourself."

"There wouldn't have been, there wasn't, until last night. I've been half expecting them to come here all morning."

"But they don't know about Tennyson, do they? Or only about the slide. Not about the bit I gave you." Then she said with something of an effort, "I think you ought to ring your Audrey: I don't see how you can stand not knowing whether he's come home or not."

"I can stand it better than I can stand speaking to his wife," he said, more sharply than he intended.

"Then why not ask the police? It can't possibly do any harm, can it? And they ought to set about finding him. What he's doing to you is horrible, let alone what he must have done to Hallam; malice like that, I mean, it's insane."

"Yes, it's horrible. During the night I wondered if it was so insane that he might even kill himself—jump in a river, for instance, when there was nobody around to see that he hadn't been pushed in—just to make it look as if there were rather a literate homicidal maniac in Bantwich. I'm literate," he said, ruefully, "and a few years ago I was a bit maniacal for a time; when I wasn't thinking of killing myself I did think of killing Harvey. It sounds impossible, but there will be doctors and people

in Bantwich who could tell Inspector Hunt about those
thoughts."

"Nick Faraday for one," she said soberly. "He's the
soul of indiscretion; anything, you know, for a laugh."

"Did he tell you about my illness last night?" Roberts
had a sudden powerful recollection of their two heads
close together in the refectory during the coffee break,
their faces turned towards him and hurriedly turned
away, while he, lily-livered coward, scuttled off to the
safe company of his old ladies.

"Yes." She had been sitting cross-legged on the edge
of his writing table, and now slipped off to stand behind
him, resting both her hands lightly on his shoulders.
"He's got a very nice wife and a lovely family but he's
one of those men who just can't bear to think a woman
might like some other man better. He seemed to know I
rather wanted you to take notice of me, even before I
knew it myself. Don't be angry with him, he's really
quite harmless."

Mr. Roberts was not so sure. And yet, and yet, the
sweetness of having this girl tell him that a man much
younger than himself, handsome too in a way Roberts
had never been, with or without his beard, with or
without the sprinkling of grey hairs his mother assured
him looked distinguished—that such a man might, out of
the simplest, crudest, jealousy disparage him, old
Roberts, seek to do him down in her eyes! He thought he
had never in his life received a greater compliment. He
basked in it until her quiet words and tone of slight
uncertainty recalled him to the complex unpleasantness
of his situation.

"I don't think," she was saying, "he'd be at all likely
to repeat what he said to me to the police. I actually
rapped him over the knuckles a bit, reminded him that he
wasn't supposed to go about telling on his patients."

"Thank you. But they'll find out of course. They'll have asked the warden about me, and he'll remember I was on sick leave the best part of a year and my post had to be forwarded to—that place." He made an effort. "Melton Hall. I don't like thinking about it even now. That's silly, I know. I've rationalised it in every way I can, but I still can't stomach the idea that I was actually out of my mind for several weeks, perhaps months."

"My dear," she said, with the same tenderness that he had put into the words some time before. "You know that it is no disgrace to be very unhappy." Her voice trembled. "There are things people need to be ashamed of, but that's not one of them, surely."

A knock at the door separated them. The English Department secretary put her head in a few inches, sniffed audibly, and announced Inspector Hunt. Hunt came in so quickly that it was clear that he did not mean to risk any refusal or attempt at delay. His glance around the room took in Nan Jones, Mr. Roberts, the typewriter with a sheet of paper still on the roller, the strip from the Chambers.

"Might I see that, Mr. Roberts? Thank you. Where exactly did you find this second—message, if that's the right word?"

"I found it," Nan said quickly. "I found it in the Chambers last night after Mr. Roberts had left our lecture room. I gave it to him later. We think it might have been typed on this machine, and I walked in here half an hour ago and nobody took any notice of me or asked what I wanted. I was in this room for at least ten minutes before Mr. Roberts came, and nobody looked in once. So anyone might have slipped in and used the typewriter."

"Thank you," Hunt said. "You've saved us some tedious questioning; as a matter of fact the note Mrs. Harvey received some weeks ago was not typed on this machine. At that time we decided to leave well enough alone. Dr. Harvey's reputation made it look as if the whole business could be classified as domestic. But since Professor Hallam's death last night we've had to change that view. We have been in touch with Mrs. Harvey."

The pause that followed was pregnant with possibilities, none of them notably pleasant. What does he expect me to say? Roberts wondered, How's old Bill? Or, so he's dead! Or, What do you expect me to say? He actually said this, as it seemed appropriate.

"What do you feel like saying?" Inspector Hunt said. Mr. Roberts felt his fists curl: Nan saw them do so, and in the midst of her dismay felt a tiny tremor of something different, perhaps relief.

"I feel like asking whether Harvey has turned up yet."

"And I must tell you that he has not, and Mrs. Harvey has heard nothing from him. We are treating the case as one of probable homicide."

Nan looked quickly from one man to the other: however obtuse this policeman might be, and she did not think he was likely to be very obtuse, he could hardly miss the sudden bleaching of Roberts' face: the finest actor at the Old Vic or Stratford could hardly have achieved that stricken look if he had known for four weeks that his old rival was dead.

"That obviously comes as a surprise to you, and an unpleasant one. Since we are investigating multiple murders we have asked for help from Scotland Yard. Superintendent Burnivel will be here this afternoon. I should be grateful if you would hold yourself available for questioning. I would like to take your typewriter again and that slip of paper. Have you any objection?"

"None that you would take any notice of."

Inspector Hunt leaned forward and read the words on the slip.

"Very appropriate, wouldn't you say, Mr. Roberts?"

"I don't know," Roberts said. Then he added, surprising himself and the others, "I don't think Harvey is dead. I think he's rather hideously and hatefully alive."

"Alive and well and living in Bantwich?" the inspector said thoughtfully. "It isn't impossible. The next few days will flush him out if your theory's correct. There will be publicity, there'll be pictures in the national press: people will claim to have seen him, and some of the claims may even be true."

"Have you a picture of him?" Nan said eagerly. "Because if he had been in the Chambers last night he'd have taken great care to keep away from Mr. Roberts, wouldn't he—but he wouldn't have worried about a complete stranger like me."

"That's a useful suggestion," Inspector Hunt said with ungrudging approval. "As a matter of fact Superintendent Burnivel is bringing with him all the recent photographs Mrs. Harvey could supply. If you are both able to come to the Chambers this afternoon you might as well look at them yourselves. How long is it since you saw Dr. Harvey, sir?"

"About four years," Roberts said. "I'd know him again anywhere; he won't have changed much in that time."

"He'd have been taking an almighty risk, then, wouldn't you say, walking in here like Mrs. Jones did just now?" Hunt said, and stretched his hand out for the typewriter. "You were glad to see her, I've no doubt. He wouldn't have expected a friendly welcome."

Roberts controlled himself and only said, "At least if any more of these little missives appear while you have my machine, you can't hold me responsible for them, can you?"

"It wouldn't be quite as simple as that, would it?" Hunt said, almost regretfully. "You might have another machine at home, you might have borrowed one yourself, you might have typed out a whole supply in advance for future use."

"Or somebody else might have," Nan said, in a dangerous tone. Then she picked up her handbag and said briskly, "Are you going to give me lunch, Rob, before we go and see the great man from London?"

"That's right," Inspector Hunt said. "No point in letting this nasty business interfere with your meals. By the way, is that the overcoat you were wearing at the Chambers last night, sir?"

The short overcoat hung on the back of the door. Roberts nodded.

"You won't mind if I just slip my hand into the pocket, will you, and see if there's anything to be found? Our constable on duty at the main doors of the Chambers last night is a very observant fellow. It was his impression that when you put your coat on to leave the building with this young lady you felt something in the pocket that caused you some disturbance. Your expression, he said, stuck in his memory. Distraught, he called it. That young man will go far."

He can't go far enough or fast enough for me, Mr. Roberts thought—impertinent pup! He said nothing: Inspector Hunt drew the little bottle out of the coat pocket between the folds of a tissue.

"You won't object to my taking this as well as your typewriter?"

"Why should I? It must have been there for years. I don't know why I haven't thrown it away."

"Yes, indeed, Mr. Roberts. All unwanted chemical substances of any sort should be washed down the lavatory or otherwise disposed of at the earliest moment, wouldn't you agree?"

"Nan," Roberts said, in sudden fierce desperation. "You're my witness, aren't you? You can see that that bottle's empty and dry, that there's nothing in it, nothing at all. I've heard of cases," he cried recklessly, "where the police have planted drugs on innocent people—"

"Have you now?" the inspector said in an easy equable tone. "Have a good look at this bottle, then, young lady, and be good enough to let me have your name and address. I want to set this gentleman's mind at ease. He seems to be taking all this very hard: almost as if he thought somebody were trying to pin something on him, wouldn't you say? First his old acquaintance Dr. Harvey, and now the police. Next thing we know he'll be thinking we're all bound up together in some sort of conspiracy, with him as the victim."

CHAPTER EIGHT

"Facts this side," Superintendent Burnivel said. "Conjectures the other. And, in any sort of scale that's worth having, one honest fact's worth half a dozen conjectures. That's my view, and it's supported by a lifetime's experience."

Inspector Hunt, who had supplied his metropolitan colleague with most of the conjectures and rather less than all of the facts, knew that he was being put in his place, but managed not to resent it. He was a quiet man, even a colourless one, but he was not without intelligence, which showed, and ambition, which he took care to conceal from his superiors.

"Fancy stuff," Burnivel said, tilting back the none too comfortable chair that Mervyn Prothero normally occupied in this room in the Chambers, at present set aside for the detectives and their patient stenographer, "comes a long way behind simple slogging footwork, as well you know. I spent an hour with Arthur Hallam's solicitor this morning. I found out two things, two facts, and I've made a few conjectures of my own, to which I won't pay a scrap more attention than I do to yours, I can assure you. Firstly, Hallam wasn't at all a wealthy man, until recently; and the money he died with hadn't been his very long."

"Who did he leave it to?"

"Whom. Watch your grammar in a place like this, you never know who might be listening. Who's through there, by the way?" The superintendent jerked his head towards the second door.

"That's the warden's room. He went home at lunch-time; he usually does, apparently, for a sleep. This is the deputy warden's, and he's moved in there for the present. The door's pretty thick."

"Good. Now, then. *Whom* Hallam left his money to was his only son and daughter in equal shares. He married a rich young woman who financed some of his travels in Asia Minor. Her parents got a bit worried and made her lock up what she had left in various trust funds for her children. She had an income for life, and when she died there was only enough for small personal legacies. He had his income from official sources, superannuation, royalties from books and so on, quite adequate, but no more. Then about six months ago he saw his solicitor about changing his will: he told Mr. Truelove that his boy and girl—they're both in their late fifties, by the way—would have something to thank their father for after all. It rankled with him, Truelove says, that the pair of them were a sight better off than their old dad, with all the accumulated funds in trust. Silly thing to worry about, wasn't it?"

Hunt, with an inward glance at his own prospects and those of his children, was inclined to agree.

"Anyway, he told Truelove that he had eighty thousand pounds to dispose of, and there might even be more. The solicitor chappie was naturally curious, but Hallam didn't offer to tell him where the lolly came from, and he thought perhaps the old man had kept a bit of loot from one of his digs and finally decided to sell it. But it makes one wonder, doesn't it?" He shot Hunt a glance under bushy eyebrows.

"Could either of the children have been in Bantwich yesterday?"

"Leaving aside," Burnivel said, "the mere conjecture as to whether any son or daughter of fifty plus would do in their dad for a half share in eighty thousand pounds when their own annual income exceeds seven thousand after tax, no, the fact is, they literally couldn't have. He's a lawyer, practices in London, was busy in court there all day yesterday, never on his own for more than a few minutes, spent the evening at home and had visitors. She's a headmistress of a girls' school in Kent: after she left school she had a meal with a friend in a private hotel, where they both live, and went on to a Parent-Teachers Association meeting, which lasted till after nine o'clock. There isn't the smallest chance that either of them did for Daddy. And they both professed astonishment this morning on hearing they had expectations—the old man hadn't told them a thing. Neither of them has any kids, by the way, if you're wondering about homicidal grandchildren: there's nothing doing with infant Hallams. So we're back with your pal Roberts, who goes round with little bottles that might have held prussic acid in his pocket and was once shut up in a bin for some considerable length of time on account of another chap's running off with his wife. And they tell us his fingerprints were on the glass that Hallam drank out of. Facts, these are."

"They weren't on the carafe," Hunt said. "That's a fact, too, and it's a fact that young Dr. Faraday told him to pick up the glass. Fool thing to do, but the doctor's not exactly quick off the mark, if you follow me."

"Unless he's very quick off the mark," Burnivel said. "Didn't you say he told you about the man Roberts being insane? He might have known about this Harvey fellow, and how the two felt about each other. Mind you, it's only conjecture, but if somebody is trying to make it look as if Roberts is a dangerous lunatic, Dr. Faraday's not in a bad position to do just that."

"Why should he? And why should he murder Hallam?"

"No reason that I can think of," Burnivel said cheerfully. "Told you conjecture would get us nowhere at this stage."

"It's a fact," Hunt now said diffidently, "that Harvey has disappeared. Nobody's had sight or sound of him in over four weeks."

"Right. And it's a fact that his wife received an envelope posted in Bantwich soon after he disappeared, and that the message inside it wasn't typed on Roberts' machine."

"Not on the one you tested anyway. But in four weeks he's had plenty of time to get rid of another machine if he'd ever had or hired one. So that's out, more or less, for certain."

"There's this second message, the one his girl friend claims to have found last night."

"This girl friend—is she all right?"

"Very nice." Inspector Hunt made a suitably eloquent sketch of her charms in mid-air. "Young widow. He's a lucky fellow."

"It's an odd time to embark on murder, just when a good-looking bird starts to make eyes at you."

"Is that a fact or conjecture?" Hunt asked demurely, and Burnivel laughed.

"You win. Not so easy to separate them in a case like this. It's a good thing the educated classes don't go in for murder on a big scale. You and I can make a good guess at how habitual criminals tick, but the possibilities get a bit out of hand when everybody connected with the case is in the ninety-eighth percentile."

"In the *what?*"

"Fact. Two percent of the population have intelligence quotients over 120. That includes anyone capable of making use of a grammar school education: and for some reason the whole lot together, whatever schooling they've had, makes up the ninety-eighth percentile."

Hunt considered himself and his own abilities and decided that he might have more in common with Roberts and Mervy Prothero and even the late Professor Hallam than he had previously guessed. Out of this rapid scrutiny he emerged with a definite idea.

"Mrs. Jones would be one of them, I should think. She's an ex-nurse, apparently, and clever with it."

"And where does that get us?"

"If someone's intelligent they generally have ordinary good sense too. If she thinks Roberts is all right, it's a point in his favour."

"Yes," Burnivel agreed, soberly, and somewhat to the local man's surprise. "Let's leave it there for the moment and think about what needs to be done."

"We'll have to find Harvey, dead or alive," Hunt said. "That's the most important thing we have to do."

"Important and fairly hopeless. If he's dead, difficult. If he's alive, with the reasons he might have for keeping himself hidden, more difficult still."

"Did he have any money on him when he disappeared? Because if he didn't he'd be running short by now."

"Or he'd be working to make some," Burnivel said thoughtfully.

"With no insurance cards?"

"Tricky: but he might be able to spin a tale—delays by his old employer, something like that. Or he could try casual labour, gardening for instance."

"Gardening at this time of year?" Hunt glanced out of

Prothero's windows at the square of bleak sky visible above the high courtyard wall.

"Dead ignorant, aren't you?" Burnivel said kindly. "Busiest time of all. Lots to be done before the winter, tidying up the shrubs and perennials, roses to be planted before the frost, pruning anything that flowers on the new wood, edges to be trimmed, tubers and corms lifted for storing, late bulbs to go in."

"You're a gardener, that's clear enough," Hunt said with grudging admiration, "but is Harvey?"

"Don't know. Nobody's asked his wife that one, but it's worth putting it to her. About the money he had on him we don't really know. She can't tell us anything about his bank account: his bank manager's as tight as a clam, won't tell us anything unless we put on the pressure. We'll have to see about that. But let's say he took a couple of hundred pounds with him—that'd last him a bit in digs, and he'd steer clear of hotels once he left London. But he'd need to look ahead, he couldn't risk being left destitute."

"There wouldn't be any risk of that if he meant to do himself in, or to provoke Roberts into doing him in."

"True enough. But that makes him dafter than Roberts, and it's Roberts who bears him a grudge, not the other way round."

They sat silent for a few minutes: then Burnivel, who was given to such intemperate gestures, pounded on the leather top of Prothero's desk with his clenched fist.

"There's something else that needs doing; checking up on everyone's movements between seven and seven-thirty yesterday evening, because, it the porter Barsted is telling the truth, the slide of the hawk and the rabbit wasn't in Professor Hallam's box when they went through the slides together at seven o'clock. It's not likely, on the face of it, that the fellow came and went twice; he's likely to have put the slide in when he poisoned the carafe; and that narrows the time down to less than half an hour."

"And it means the murderer must have got in through the door to the yard," Hunt said at once; for though taken aback by his senior colleague's rapid grasp of a time relationship he hadn't himself fully appreciated, he had no intention of being outstripped in interpreting its significance. "And that means," he added triumphantly, "our murderer must know the building pretty well. It's a pointer to Roberts, if you like."

"I don't like," Burnivel said crossly. "Such evidence as we've got against him is entirely circumstantial: he hadn't a ghost of a motive for doing Hallam in, as far as I can see. Unless the lab tells us there're traces of cyanide in that little bottle, we haven't a leg to stand on. At this stage I could make out a better case against Harvey."

"Harvey wouldn't know his way round this place."

"He might. People come and go here all day, Dr. Bentley makes a point of that in the statement you took from him. He's had four weeks to assume a different name, sign on for a class every night if he felt like it."

"The porters would notice, wouldn't they, if somebody kept coming in and out?"

"Let's ask them."

They sent for Wilson. His answer was disconcerting.

"Lord love you, we've got some people who practically live here! Retired folk, a few eccentrics like Miss Blount, everybody knows her, housewives with grown-up children and time on their hands, you'd be surprised. Four or five courses at a time, some of them take, and they come and go at all hours. It's warm and comfortable, rather like a club. They can be sure of meeting friends, you see, and in our refectory the waitresses don't cough and frown at them because they want the tables cleared."

"These last four weeks has anyone seemed to be hanging around that you haven't noticed before? Anyone who was here for certain yesterday evening?"

"In four weeks, sir, and at the beginning of the academic year when there's a great many new students anyhow, I don't think we would notice anybody in particular—except a very nice-looking young woman, like that Mrs. Jones. It takes a long time for an impression to build up, if you follow me." Wilson was choosing his words with great care. A greatly increased sense of his own dignity had come to him since he had realised that he held a position of trust in an institution now nationally notorious. His photograph had appeared with Barsted's in the national dailies, holding up the slide of the hawk under the headline "Lethal Literary Lunatic at Large?" The literariness had wiped off on Wilson and he was determined not to lose an opportunity of sustaining his character.

"A man," Burnivel said. "Almost certainly a man: wouldn't a man, new to the place, coming in and out every day, be more likely to be noticed than a woman?"

Wilson gave quite a convincing impression of a seeker after truth deeply engaged in thought, and finally admitted that, yes, a man would possibly show up, especially if he were under retirement age.

"But I can't say I've noticed anyone myself," he finished.

"Have a look at these pictures," Burnivel said, fishing a handful of photographs out of a folder. "Do you recognise that chap at all?"

Wilson performed further putative mental contortions, but shook his head.

"But that doesn't mean he hasn't been here," he

hastened to add. "It isn't a distinguished face, you see, not like Dr. Bentley's or Mr. Baird's now, or Dr. Faraday's. Not a face you'd pick out in a crowd, would you say?"

Burnivel grunted noncommittally and dismissed him.

"I asked Mr. Roberts and his young woman to drop in and have a look at those pictures this afternoon," Hunt said. "She had the rather bright idea that if Dr. Harvey was in the building at all last night he'd have kept well away from Roberts, but wouldn't have worried about a complete stranger like herself."

"Good sense. I look forward to meeting Mrs. Jones. In the meantime, there are two jobs you must get your chaps on to."

"They're questioning all the photographic departments in the city to try to find out where that slide came from."

"Good," Burnivel said, but was nevertheless perceptibly displeased at having the wind taken out of his sails: Hunt made a note that his London colleague didn't greatly care for intelligent anticipation. "You won't guess the other, I shouldn't think."

"Not if I can help it, Hunt told himself drily, and made his mind a convenient blank.

"We've got to look into the likely sources for Professor Hallam's windfall; I've a man going round the London salesrooms, incidentally, checking up on recent sales of antiquities and so forth. But I don't think we'll strike lucky there; if he'd been holding on to something worth that sort of money for thirty years, it's not likely that he'd have been able to keep it a secret, or that he'd have wanted to; he seems to have been rather a showy old character. And leaving it till he was eighty before cashing in would be risky; he might have popped off without finding out what he could get for it at today's inflated prices."

"Could he have won on the pools?" Hunt suggested.

"Maybe." Burnivel sounded unconvinced. "Difficult to imagine that sort of chap posting his coupons—and again, wouldn't he have talked about it?"

"That's conjecture," Hunt said, somewhat primly.

"It's *reasonable* conjecture," Burnivel said, after a moment's consideration and a not too friendly glance at the younger man. "If his old friends think he's an exhibitionist of sorts, and he didn't mention this windfall to anybody, it suggests to me that there was something shady about this money, something he wasn't too proud of."

"If he'd sold something to an overseas buyer without a licence?"

"My fellow who's checking on the salesrooms will know all about that. But I rather doubt if he'd have gone straight to his solicitor to alter his will in that case. Shady, I said, not illegal."

"Yes. I suppose there's a difference?"

"For people like that there is. Just as it's shady to send a lady a scrap of poetry through the post with no explanation given, but she'd have the devil of a job persuading anybody she was sufficiently bothered by it for it to constitute a nuisance, in the legal sense."

"This Mrs. Harvey—how's she taking the loss of her husband?"

"Hard to say. Our chap in Cambridge, when he first disappeared, said she didn't seem so much concerned or frightened as annoyed: seems he'd been off on several long weekends with various young ladies, students some of them. He thought she was more bothered about the letter and the chance that her first husband was somehow involved than she was about the second one going off."

"Here's husband number one now, I should think," Hunt interrupted, as his constable opened the door to

usher in Roberts and Nan Jones. Rain had begun to fall
and her yellow hair—the real thing, Burnivel decided,
running a practiced eye over the pair of them—was damp
over the crown of her head; her fringe stuck in wisps to
her brow so that it would hardly have been surprising to
hear that she was the daughter of this slight, bearded,
grizzled man, who marched in with a show of considerably more confidence than Burnivel judged him at
all likely to be feeling.

"Mr. Roberts? I am Superintendent Burnivel of
Scotland Yard. I was last here in 1951 or '52, if my
memory serves me rightly, looking into a little crime at
the local children's hospital. Were you here then?"

Roberts shook his head. "No, I was in the Navy. I was
born in Bantwich and read for my first degree here: then I
was called up. I was demobbed in 1953."

"And when were you at Cambridge?"

"For five years, from 1960."

"And was this picture taken during those years?"

Burnivel held up a photograph. It showed two young
men wearing the stupid grins of those who have been
instructed to smile when they would rather be doing
something else. The something else was fairly clear: they
were on a riverbank, there were willows, reeds and a
boat. One of the frustrated anglers was bearded, one was
clean-shaven. Nan Jones, peering over Roberts' shoulder
said in amazement, "How much you've changed—I'd
never have recognised you."

"That's Harvey," Roberts said. "I hadn't a beard then.
Yes," he said to Burnivel, "that was soon after we met,
and just before I was married. So it was probably the
summer of 1960."

"That confirms what Mrs. Harvey told us. This is
more recent, about two years ago; he'd had his beard off,
as you see."

"It makes a difference," Roberts said.

"Yes. Would you recognise him as he is now, do you think?"

"I think so. I can't be sure. He's put on weight, as well as shaving, and his hair's begun to go thin at the temples. If he walked in here now and said who he was, I think I might say, how little you've changed. But it wouldn't be true. He's changed a great deal."

"You mean," Burnivel said heavily, "this man might have passed you in the street or on a staircase and you wouldn't immediately have said to yourself, that's Harvey."

"That's what I mean. Especially as I didn't know he'd shaved."

"And you, Mrs. Jones. Have you seen this man in the last four weeks?"

Nan shook her head in simple disappointment. "No, I haven't."

"In four weeks he might have grown a beard again," Hunt said.

"I shouldn't think so," Roberts said with surprising conviction. "It took me longer than that and his hair's lighter and finer than mine."

"He wouldn't be likely to grow one for disguise if he didn't want Mr. Roberts to recognise him," Burnivel said. "He'd be safer staying clean-shaven. We're no further on. Assuming this old friend of yours is still alive, sir"—he turned to Roberts with that sudden change of voice and manner Hunt had already found disconcerting—"what do you think he's likely to do next?"

"Come forward and give himself up, perhaps?"

"That's a possibility, but a very remote one, I'd say. It's a formidable thing he's taken on himself if he's a free agent, slipping away and staying in hiding while some-

body plays literary parlour games and commits murder—
unless of course that somebody is Dr. Harvey himself."

"He'd have to be insane to kill a complete stranger
like Hallam just for the sake of a sort of monstrous pun."

"He would have to be insane, I agree; or much
concerned to prove that someone else was."

"Yes, or that," Roberts said steadily enough.

"I'm glad we see eye to eye. And a sort of"—but this
time the right term eluded Burnivel and he frowned,
snapping his fingers as though the words might emerge if
summoned from the air of Prothero's study—"a sort of
obsession with elegies, or whatever they're called,
seems to be this character's hallmark. Was Dr. Harvey
much attracted to elegies, would you say?"

"No more than anyone else with an interest in
occasional poetry."

"Occasional poetry?" Burnivel echoed with lifted
eyebrows.

"Poetry written for special occasions: anniversaries,
weddings, funerals, what have you."

"What we have," Burnivel said in a tone laden with
meaning, "is a funeral, possibly more than one funeral."
He was silent for a moment; then a thought struck him.
"Like the bits the Poet Laureate turns out when the
Queen goes off to Australia or something?"

"The last Poet Laureate," Mr. Roberts said. "The
present one doesn't do it."

"Why not?" Burnivel said in righteous indignation.
"It's what he's paid for, isn't it?"

"It's generally considered an anachronism," Roberts
said in exactly the reasonable tone Nan Jones had heard
him use to Miss Blount, Mrs. Landor, Mr. Bell; and the
sound of it warmed her instantly and assured her that
whatever the fantastic possibilities of the situation they
found themselves in—policemen, poison, prison dis-
mayingly in the background—this man was perfectly

sane, if by sanity one were to understand the capacity to adapt, to adjust, to use one's adult judgement to choose between different responses and pick the one calculated to preserve the civilised decencies.

"Wasn't Tennyson the Poet Laureate?" Burnivel said, surprising himself almost as much as the others.

"Yes, indeed."

"He wrote this *In Memoriam* thing for a chap called Arthur Hallam?"

"Yes."

"Are there many more of them? Poems like that?"

"Elegies, you mean? In English?"

"English will do, to be going on with."

"A few famous ones. Dozens that are hardly known."

"But a scholar like Harvey would know them?"

"Certainly."

"And you too, Mr. Roberts?"

"Harvey was a poet himself, and a tremendous reader with a good memory. Prose fiction's my speciality, I read poetry mainly for pleasure and for my students' sake."

"So you wouldn't be able to tell us of any other likely victims for a man with an obsession"—this time Burnivel produced the word with pleased conviction—"of this gloomy sort?"

"Other people, you mean, with the same names as men and women who've been important enough to have dirges written for them?"

"Something of the kind. Because if there should be anyone in that position we could keep an eye on them, you see—just in case."

"Yes," Mr. Roberts said. The reasonable voice had gone. He sounded so stricken that Nan looked at him in something like dismay. He was sitting on a low chair that Hunt had indicated to him on their arrival—she sat on its arm, with her hand resting lightly on his shoulder: now she let her fingers tighten reassuringly. Burnivel was warning him, she realised that, she knew that he realised it too. He was actually giving information while he pretended to be asking for it; a dirty trick, she thought indignantly—but then poisoning people was dirtier still, and if this London detective thought Rob was capable of that it was fair enough to try to protect any further victim.

"So if there's anything that comes to your mind offhand—" Burnivel was saying.

"Gray wrote a dirge for a favourite cat drowned in a tub of goldfish."

"I am serious, Mr. Roberts."

"So am I. You asked me about elegies in the English language. That's one of the most famous. John Donne wrote two magnificent threnodies for a young girl called Elizabeth Drury, and several others, including one for Prince Henry."

"There aren't many princes around."

"Not in Bantwich," Roberts agreed; and Nan saw that he had regained his precarious poise, and that it was being on his home ground that had helped him to this better state. "There could be an Elizabeth Drury, though."

Burnivel had already written the name down; it dawned on the others that a woman of that name, living perhaps within a few miles of where they now sat, might be in actual danger.

"Any others?"

Roberts frowned. "'Adonais'—Shelley's elegy for Keats. I suppose that's the best known of all—certainly as famous as *In Memoriam*."

"John Keats, the poet?" Burnivel asked, and when Roberts nodded, "Keats isn't a common name."

"'Lycidas,'" Roberts said slowly. "Milton; for a young clergyman who was drowned in the Irish Channel.

I can't remember his name, though. I think it isn't usually printed with the title."

A firm, even peremptory, knock on the communicating door announced Mervyn Prothero, who was apparently disinclined to be kept out of his own room even after generously offering it to Hunt for his temporary headquarters.

"You'll excuse me," the deputy warden said to the company at large. "I have to collect some papers for a lecture at four-fifteen. I have waited as long as possible buy I really cannot delay my departure any further."

"Prothero," Roberts said, and it was obvious to Nan if to none of the others that he had almost forgotten the terrible context in which he made his query in the disinterested curiosity of the man who can generally find a word or an attribution without hesitating for more than a moment. " 'Lycidas'—what was the name of the young man it was written for?"

Prothero stopped in the very act of stuffing papers into his briefcase.

"A very fine poem. Milton is vastly underrated at the moment. We have Leavis to thank for that, as well as for better things. *Grate on their scrannel pipes*—splendid stuff, full of vigour. Brilliantly sustained too, wouldn't you say?"

"Yes, I would. What was the boy's name?"

Prothero considered. "Something quite commonplace, I believe. There is a collected shorter poems of Milton in my bookcase, third shelf down."

His bustling hurry seemed to have abated, he unlocked the bookcase and took out a small leatherbound volume.

"Ah, yes, here it is. Edward King. An ordinary name."

CHAPTER NINE

An ordinary name, certainly; but the effect it produced on Superintendent Burnivel and Inspector Hunt seemed to Mr. Roberts at the time astonishing, and was brought vividly to his mind when he entered his familiar lecture room in the Chambers the following Tuesday; for just as the members of his class—which was full on this occasion, flatteringly full even, since the weather showed no signs of improving—turned to each other and began to talk in low murmurs as he walked to the lecturer's desk and got out his notes, so that Wednesday afternoon of the preceding week those two policemen, at the mention of Edward King, lost to all outward appearances their interest in him and in Hallam, speaking together in low excited voices. Nan had leant forward quite unashamedly, but she could hear nothing and had turned to Roberts with a look of perplexity that might have been reflected off his own features. Only Mervyn Prothero, having unintentionally set some kind of cat among the pigeons, seemed quite indifferent to its effects, and apparently only then recollected the urgency of his errand.

"You'll excuse me, I'm sure," he said, for the second time in five minutes, "I really must go, now, this minute. Unless I am needed here?"

Burnivel had made some sort of perceptible effort to

recollect the deputy warden's identity and purposes, then nodded a brusque dismissal. Prothero took himself off; Roberts had risen and held out his hand to Nan.

"If you've finished with us for the moment, perhaps we could go too?"

But Burnivel then shook his head.

"Mrs. Jones may leave whenever she wishes, but there are further questions I have to ask you, Mr. Roberts."

"I'll stay," Nan had said. "May I stay, please?"

"If Mr. Roberts has no objection."

"Would there be any point to my objecting to anything?"

Burnivel had looked at him closely, then repeated his headshake with a different emphasis.

"I wouldn't advise you to take that line, Mr. Roberts; my colleague here has told me that you show a slight disposition to resent questioning, a slight reluctance to assist us in the performance of our duty. That's a very mistaken attitude, I assure you. We're only too anxious to get to the bottom of these unpleasant—happenings." Burnivel had paused, obviously rather pleased at his use of the bang-up-to-date term. "And since you assure us you have been no more than a bystander, maybe even a victim, of somebody's nasty sense of fun you must be as eager as we are to see Professor Hallam's murderer caught."

"Of course I am."

"And Dr. Harvey found, so that he can be restored to your—I beg your pardon, *his* wife."

Roberts had said nothing.

"And you will be at least as keen to tell us, as we are to know, exactly where you were between ten o'clock in the evening and five o'clock in the morning of Thursday October 16 and Friday October 17 of this year. Shortly

after five o'clock on the seventeenth, a young man called
Edward King was found stabbed to death on a building
site in Nottingham."

"Have you all read *The Moonstone* now?" Mr.
Roberts asked in a louder voice than usual, louder than
was actually necessary, for the chatter had subsided,
though faces were still averted, mostly demurely bent
over the pages of Wilkie Collins, as if in a last-minute
revision of the text. There was a stray cough or two; Mr.
Roberts looked along the rows without encountering any
eyes but Nan's. He had half expected that she would stay
away; he had not seen her since that dreadful session of
pointed question and meandering incoherent answer. For,
of course, he couldn't remember anything about that
particular evening: Thursdays had no special significance
for him. His mother sometimes, not always, attended
meetings of the Townswomen's Guild; as far as he could
say, offhand, he had gone home as usual, eaten his
evening meal, gone to his study and read, written or
corrected the first essays of the new session. He thought
it unlikely that he would have gone out, knew that he
would remember a theatre or cinema or a concert as he
seldom attended any of those functions, imagined—
imagined? Burnivel had said severely, it's information I
want, not fancies!—believed, then, that it had been a
Thursday night like any other, was almost sure in
retrospect that his mother had been away. Then could he
produce anybody who could substantiate his statement,
make it certain for instance that he hadn't, in the course
of the evening, taken out his car and driven the thirty-
two miles to Nottingham? No, it was only his word for
it, and obviously his word could never be enough for
them, when they were already convinced he couldn't tell
fact from fancy, was to all intents and purposes deluded,

wasn't that what they thought? He had looked from Burnivel to Hunt, hearing in his own words, his own tone, precisely those intimations of singularity he knew they would be seeking. And at last, to bring matters to a head, he had got up, he had asked them whether they would be making a charge, and when, after a moment's colloquy with his junior, Burnivel had shaken his head, he had said to Nan simply but firmly, "I think you should go home now. That's what I shall do. If you want me, that's where I shall be." Neither the police nor Mrs. Jones had wanted him, evidently. He had excused himself from his daytime work at the university on the Thursday and Friday because he was sure that something would happen and he preferred that it should happen quietly on his own territory, though the dread of his mother's reaction, the shock she would suffer, disturbed him more than the exigencies of his ordinary departmental duties might have done. But the weekend had come and gone, on Monday he had gone back to work. He thought that perhaps he was being watched: then he thought that perhaps to think that was a sort of illness. Through his considerable dull apprehension he could also feel the sharper ache of loss. Coming into the lecture room had been the worst thing he had had to do yet, coming in with the certainty that she would not be there. But there she was, with a look upon her face that was nowhere near a smile, but at which he nevertheless managed to smile himself: for it was concern her face showed, unmistakably, and he knew at once that if she had not written or rung, it must have been for very good reasons.

He began to talk about Collins; he had prepared this lecture years before for a meeting of the Guild of Undergraduates, a semisocial occasion for which anything too serious would have been a solecism. It was good, meaty stuff, it was fluent, capable and humorous. Whatever assortment of emotions his twenty-three ladies and two men had brought into the room, by the time he had talked for three quarters of an hour, cheerful amusement prevailed, in the teeth of considerable odds. They were delighted, his class, with his account of the relationship, personal and professional, between Collins and Dickens; the talk was generally laced and lightened with anecdotes, and when he got down to *The Moonstone* itself and read some passages aloud, there were appreciative murmurs. They find it interesting, Mr. Roberts mused, distancing himself a little as he read them Lady Verinder's dismissal of Sergeant Cuff, and assured them that in the 1840s this was entirely feasible; but no, perhaps it's me they find interesting: though after all there has been very little in the newspapers, just one or two references to a possible link between Harvey's disappearance and Hallam's murder with a mention of the odd fact that Mrs. Harvey's former husband is a well-known—huh!—figure in Bantwich academic circles. Not much to get one's teeth into, all things considered, and my old ladies could surely never bring themselves to believe they've actually sat down in the refectory and drunk coffee with a mad murderer. Though somebody must have done that, or something like it, somebody must actually know the man who poisoned Hallam and stabbed that builders' labourer on a bit of waste ground near a pub not forty miles from here. I suppose Hunt or Burnivel, or one of their men, is showing pictures of me to the pub-keeper and the poor chap's friends and asking them if they've ever seen that face before. Well, I just hope they've shown them Harvey's picture too. Fair's fair, and that bastard's made trouble enough for me. Why can't he show up, why can't they find him? For since I know I didn't kill those two, surely he must have? Who else would have strewn ivy and laurel leaves over a lad's body, even if he couldn't run to myrtles brown? And, while he listened to Miss Blount gently rambling on about the death of Mr. Tulkinghorn in *Bleak House*— "we shall probably talk about Dickens in a week or two, Miss Blount"—he had mildly pointed out, but she was not to be stopped in full flood—he let her kindness and her irrelevance wash soothingly over him and heard, under her voice, Burnivel's edgy London snarl intoning the first words of Milton's poem in a way that suggested he found the elegy a sort of insult.

> Yet once more, O ye laurels, and once more
> Ye myrtles brown, with ivy never sere . . .

Laurels and ivy, the Nottingham police hadn't been able to make head or tail out of that. They thought perhaps a child or a half-wit of some kind might have found the body and tried to make a sort of funeral rite. "Or immigrants, we thought, they could have a sort of cult, it might have been blood sacrifice. Or hippies, but then you'd have expected hemp leaves, I suppose. Or fig leaves." At which stroke of wit Burnivel had roared briefly and Hunt had managed a convincing smile. Mr. Roberts had not. Then the superintendent had undergone one of his lightning changes of mood. "So here's this lad dead, not yet twenty, just come into a few hundred pounds on the Premium Bonds; parents distracted, his girl half crazy, just to satisfy some screwy intellectual with a taste for the macabre. Not very pretty in my opinion, Mr. Roberts. And not very clever, either, for a man with a good brain. Or the remains of one."

Miss Blount's voice became softer and softer, the pauses between her words longer and longer, she sank into the semblance of a gentle sleep. As Mr. Roberts prepared to bring the first part of the evening to a close, she sat up suddenly to remark, "It was their both being ladies that confused me. Lady Dedlock and Lady Verinder, I mean. People had such respect for a title in those days. Young Arthur quite set his heart on a knighthood," she said gaily, now evidently fully awake, "and poor Charity was rather disappointed as year after year came and went; she had looked forward so much to being Lady Hallam. I think in some ways she was just a little inclined to be a snob."

She does not quite know where she is, Mr. Roberts thought. She is wandering a little; how am I to bring her back without letting her know how far behind she has left us? And he said at once, before the mystified glances of his other students could disconcert her, "You are absolutely right, Miss Blount, to couple Lady Dedlock and Lady Verinder in that way. Collins and Dickens had much the same approach to the depiction of upper class characters. They knew their readers liked something to goggle at."

"My friend Charity would have liked us all to goggle at her," Miss Blount said in great good humour and apparently in full possession of herself and her situation, and Mr. Roberts at once suggested that they should go upstairs for refreshment: a cup of coffee might keep her going for the rest of the evening, clearly she was in need of some mild stimulant. He saw her into the charge of Mr. Peachment, with a remark to that effect, when he was sure the old lady would not hear.

"A very mild stimulant," Mr. Peachment said. "It tells you in the textbooks that a medium-sized cup of coffee has five grains of caffeine in it: I'd guess the stuff they sell us here has about two grains, on a good day."

"It's hot and wet," Mr. Roberts said mechanically, for he was longing to be with Nan, who had gone upstairs a long way ahead of him and reached the serving end of the counter while he talked to Mr. Peachment. Then he saw her signalling to him, with a cup and saucer in each hand and a packet of biscuits grasped by the corner of its cellophane wrapping between her teeth. "Would you excuse me, Mr. Peachment?" He took a cup and saucer from her and thought that he must not ask her why she hadn't attempted to get in touch with him, as if he had even the slightest right to imagine that she might have done: but as though his unspoken question was already in her ears, she said at once, before they had time to move away from the queue and sit down, "Oh, if you knew how I've been longing to see you—it's been the longest week I've ever spent."

"There's a table over by the window," Mr. Roberts said, "if you don't mind the draught."

"Bother the draught—I was afraid you'd think I was, you know, cutting you dead. Oh, God, what a thing to say, I'm awfully sorry—" But she laughed, she laughed, and he knew that she could never ever have produced the literally shocking metaphor if she'd been for a moment capable of imagining him plunging a knife into that boy in Nottingham, and his relief was so great that he had to laugh as well, and then he could at last ask, "Why didn't you ring me? I wanted you so badly."

"It was Davy—honestly, nothing else would have kept me away. If I hadn't been able to come tonight I would have rung or written or something. He's been ill; when I got home on Wednesday he was a bit touchy and cross, and Mum and I had rather a row. I thought she'd been letting him play up, you know how grannies simply let children have their own way all the time, so it was a miserable evening, I can tell you, and I nearly rang then; and then I thought I'd better not, I thought I might be going too fast for you, you know, being younger and everything. So I didn't, and Davy woke up with a temperature and actually he had to go into hospital, he had a virus pneumonia. He's all right now, but of course I had to stay with him all the time, I didn't go home at all until this evening; and Mum said I should have a break tonight, she'd go and sit with him till he goes to sleep. He'll be home in a day or two, certainly by the weekend. Oh, and when he was really bad and I got rather low and weepy, I told Mum all about you."

She paused for breath. "Being older and everything?" Mr. Roberts said.

"Yes, everything. All the queer horrid things that have been happening and might happen."

"Was she very worried?"

"Not very: she said, 'Oh, Nan, you do pick 'em.'" She screwed up her face, and Mr. Roberts could hear her mother's tone of rueful resignation, though he had never so much as spoken to her on the telephone. "So I said you would never drive when you were drunk, and you were nice to old ladies. That did it; honestly the way Mum talks you'd think she was Miss Blount's older sister. She wants you to come for Sunday tea and meet Davy, and she thinks you ought to bring your mother, too."

Roberts said carefully, "You told her about the police and Harvey and the Nottingham murder and everything?"

"Everything. She says obviously a loony did it, and nothing I'd told her made it sound as if you were a loony. Not now, anyway."

"I might be," Mr. Roberts said, astonishing himself, "every time there's a full moon or something. I shouldn't joke about it," he added scrupulously. "I never thought I could possibly joke about it."

"Yes, it's in awfully bad taste. Mum says I make the most awful jokes. It's the generation gap or something.

Can you really bear me?" Most of his class were on their feet, putting down cups and saucers on the low refectory table with a meaningful clatter, as they prepared to return to the lecture room. So he could only look at her. "Yes, that'll do," she said. "Come on, educate me. It'll be a long job, I'm warning you."

"It can last a lifetime as far as I'm concerned," Roberts said.

Miss Blount had drunk her coffee at surprising speed, wiped her lips on a tiny handkerchief and gone downstairs ahead of Mrs. Berg and Mrs. Landor. "I have a tiny private matter to attend to," she remarked to those good ladies, who were inclined to hover over her solicitously. They exchanged glances, they reached the same conclusion; and judging, rightly, that she would be offended if they offered to accompany her to the ladies' cloakroom, returned to their seats while she trotted off downstairs, though to quite another destination; it was to the warden's office that she made her way, bumping into Humphrey Baird as she passed him in the corridor.

"I'm so sorry, Miss Blount, I can't have been looking where I was going."

"Not at all, Mr. Baird. It was my own judgement that was at fault. My eyesight is not what it has been. This is Dr. Bentley's door, I believe?"

"Yes, indeed."

"And am I right in thinking that he has a very fine canvas of my old friend Charity Snettisloe's hanging over his fireplace?"

"Very fine indeed," Baird said, and then quieted his conscience by murmuring, "if one cares for that sort of thing."

"I thought I would just like to take a little look at it, if Dr. Bentley would have no objection."

"I'm sure he wouldn't object in the least—indeed, he's never here on a Tuesday evening. I'll knock on his door, but I've no doubt he's left the building."

He knocked. Surprisingly, in view of what he had just been saying, there were sounds within, but no voice bade them enter. Baird knocked again, turning a puzzled face to the old lady. The sounds increased, became to his fairly acute ear discernibly those of large objects being moved, pushed, shifted, scraped. He opened the door a fraction and called, "Warden?"

"Baird? Is that you, Baird?"

Mervyn Prothero came to the door; he wore no jacket, his shirt sleeves were rolled up, his face was a duskier red than usual and beaded with tiny drops of sweat.

"Perhaps you could—I was just about to ring for Barsted, but since you are here, if you would be so good—oh, Miss Blount, I failed to see you. That corridor is poorly lit."

Miss Blount pushed gently past Baird and into the book-lined room: her usual mildly bemused look gave way to a deeper, more marked confusion.

"Is this not the warden's room, Mr. Prothero?"

"Yes, of course, dear lady, and I would not be here if the police investigating Professor Hallam's sad death had not turned me out of my own, for the moment."

Miss Blount ignored this; it was not Prothero's presence that had disturbed her, though for a moment it had shaken Humphrey Baird.

"Because," she went on, as if the deputy warden had not spoken, "I have been in here at Dr. Bentley's invitation more than once and I recall, I thought I recalled quite clearly, a great picture of spring, with Persephone and her attendants dancing to the pipes of Pan, above the overmantel."

"You are perfectly right, Miss Blount. And it is that

very picture that has just caused me some distress. Baird, dear chap, would you be so very kind?"

It was not easy to understand what must have happened. Above the fireplace was a faded patch of wallpaper, an expanse rather, so vast had been this product of Mrs. Hallam's youthful toil. And that labour of love, frame and all, now rested against the warden's desk, some feet away. By the fireplace was an assemblage of chairs and a set of library steps.

"It slipped," Prothero said succinctly. "It fell. It is astonishing that so little damage was done."

Baird exclaimed, looking at the size of the picture, "Surely you can't have been so"—he paused for a tactful epithet to replace the word *idiotic*, the first that had come to his mind—"so determined to manage on your own that you actually tried to put it back yourself?"

Prothero looked sheepish, spreading his hands in a little deprecatory gesture. The hands were dirty; it could easily be conceived how rarely in the course of a year a cleaner would dust the top of Persephone's frame. Baird just registered that one of the fingers, as well as being dusty, bore a dark stain, something shiny, sticky, black; at the same moment he became aware of how cold the room was, in spite of the central heating. The shutters were open, the windows gaping wide.

"Stuffy," Prothero said, following his gaze. "Like a little fresh air myself. Fresh air and exercise, that's the way to keep young, eh, Miss Blount? That's why I tried to put the ladies back on the wall myself," he went on rapidly, "independence, the healthy life. But since I really must confess I could hardly lift the thing, I must sacrifice my independence, Baird, and beg you to assist me. Perhaps you will take this end, I will take the other."

Baird assisted him: the painting was not actually as heavy as he would have guessed. It had no glass, for one thing, and the backing seemed to be the thinnest matchboard. Only the frame was massive, and it was the frame's dimensions rather than its weight that would have made it awkward for only one man to handle. The slender chain by which it had been suspended was intact. On the faded area of the chimney breast two picture-hanging nails were driven in.

"I wonder why it fell? The nails seem pretty firm to me," Baird said, testing the one nearest to him from a safe position on the library steps.

"Ah, I hammered them back into position a moment before you and Miss Blount here came to my rescue. Otherwise I would hardly have attempted to replace the picture: why, it might have come down again."

Baird and Prothero rearranged the furniture. All was neat, all was normal. Miss Blount stood on the hearth-rug, gazing up at her friend's creation.

"A great deal of work has gone into that picture," she said, nodding her head in approval. "I have only one criticism to make. The nymphs, the goddess, are quite lovely. But I cannot understand why a married woman should have been so coy in the representation of the god Pan."

"Was she married when she painted it?" Baird asked, feeling that he should show some interest.

"Oh yes, yes. If you look at the signature you will see quite clearly: the initials are C.H., H for Hallam."

But they were not, they were C.S., S for Snettisloe. Porthero shook his head, firmly but kindly.

"I think you will find you are mistaken, dear lady. Even after her marriage Mrs. Hallam continued to sign her canvasses with the initials of her maiden name."

"Not this one," Miss Blount said. "I was with her the day she finished it. C.S., she painted on it; as soon as she saw what she had done she gave a little squeal. 'Talking-to you of the old days, Griselda, that's what made me do it—I've signed it as if you and I were just girls together.' And then she changed it, changed it to C.H. That was why I wanted to see it again tonight," Miss Blount said severely. "It is the only picture of hers for which I feel any sentimental attachment."

She left them. Baird looked at Prothero, who spread his hands wide. And while he thus reminded the younger man, who needed no reminding, of Miss Blount's age and the unreliability of her memory, the increasing tenuousness of her grasp upon real events, Baird's eyes could not help straying to the black streak on Prothero's finger, and from there to the initials on the corner of the huge, overpopulated canvas above the mantelshelf; nor could he quite dismiss the faint sense of unease Prothero's strange preference for cold night air had awoken in him a few moments back, or the strangeness of the deputy warden's pointless prevarication. Odd noises enough he, and perhaps Miss Blount, had heard from the far side of Dr. Bentley's door, but the tap of a hammer replacing a nail had surely not been among them.

CHAPTER TEN

The following Sunday was fine. Mr. Roberts drove his mother to Nan's parents' house early in the afternoon; this was at Nan's suggestion. "Let them look each other over while we're not there to embarrass them. And we'll go and fetch Davy home; that ought to put you in his good books. You'll be a sort of St. George delivering him from the dragon." "I couldn't possibly live up to that sort of image," he protested. "You're saintly enough for anything; and I bet you could slay dragons if you had to," she said with imperturbable assurance. Somebody else, that's whom she's fallen in love with; she's a child herself, showering all the qualities she admires on the people she likes, Mr. Roberts thought with mingled exasperation and delight. And while he sat in the waiting room in the great dreary hospital building and waited for her to dress the little boy and bring him down, he found himself thinking of his former wife, who had never even for one moment credited him with abilities greater than he possessed. He had thought that that might have preserved Audrey from disillusionment: it had not. His failure to attain, or even to attach much importance to, the trivial goals she had thought well within his reach, and Harvey's insolence of achievement, these were favourite themes in the period of their increasing estrangement. Yet he hadn't done so badly, after all; his own modest ambitions to be a sound teacher, a friend to his students, a support to his mother, had all been fulfilled. He had nothing to be ashamed of except the hurt that man and woman had dealt him, and now he would be in a fair way to forgive them both if it weren't for the reawakening of his old self-mistrust in the face of recent happenings.

He picked up an old, old magazine and put it down again. The waiting room held only himself and a young man, a father, he supposed, though he hardly looked old enough for such a venerable role, with a sleeping infant on the crook of his arm. The boy caught his eye and smiled.

"Here, hold her for a minute, would you? I'm perishing for a fag. Think they'd mind?"

"I shouldn't think so," Mr. Roberts said. "There's an ashtray on that table, so they expect people to smoke." He held his arms out and received the baby, who barely stirred at her change of guardian. It was clearly a girl, layers of pink knitting with crocheted frills left no room for doubt.

"Sit down, why don't you?" the young man said, lighting his cigarette. "She's heavier'n she looks, you'll find out."

Mr. Roberts sat down.

"Your kid ill?"

"No, I haven't any. I brought a friend to fetch her little boy home."

"Oh. Well, thanks. I'll take her now."

Mr. Roberts handed the baby over: this time its face puckered, its eyes opened, then closed on a long sighing breath. The two men's eyes met, a smile of relief passed between them as it became clear that the child would not cry. Nan and I might have a child, Mr. Roberts realised.

Audrey never wanted children. I wonder if she has any now? I wonder if they are fatherless?

The minutes passed, the young man's wife appeared with another child, they greeted each other and left the room, the young man just grinning back at him. Left to himself Mr. Roberts' slight sense of elevation fled; he began to feel lonely, bored, useless. A row of potted plants on the windowsill offered more interest than the torn and crumpled periodicals on the table. He got up and looked at them: under a fine luxuriant fern there were little piles of dark seeds, like droppings, he thought, as if the fern were an animal. *The strutting fern lay seeds on the windowsill* . . . whether Dylan Thomas is generally overrated or not, whether or not *Under Milk Wood* is worth any serious critical attention, that's a good poem; arguably his personal best: "In Memory of Ann Jones."

"Here we are," her voice said behind him, a bit too brightly, he considered, realising that she was awkward, she was strained, wanting this first meeting to be more of a success than there was any real likelihood of its being. And, because he was stunned and sick at the new fear his active mind had unleashed, he couldn't manage the easy smile or the reassuring pat on the head he'd supposed would meet the case. "Well, David," was all he could say, and not in a very cheerful tone at that. "I'm sorry you haven't been well. I've come to drive you and your mother home." St. George! he thought disgustedly, holding the car door open for them: I've enough to do with my own dragons. But Nan noticed no deficiency, smiled at him with what he took to be divine charity, nodded approval. "Don't try to rush things," she had told him on the way to the hospital. "He'll be suspicious at first: just give him time. He's a friendly little boy as a rule, but being away is bound to have upset him a bit."

Being away had certainly upset him: though Mr.

Roberts had no idea what standards of behaviour were acceptable in a two-year-old—and he doubted whether his mother could recall that period of his own infancy with any clearness—the hours they spent together before Davy's bedtime were curiously dreadful. Nan's mother and father were kind, tactful, full of diversions and distractions: Mrs. Roberts veiled her own formidable personality in an impenetrable austerity of demeanour, refusing cake, refusing even sugar in her tea, as if these harmless indulgences of the flesh might lead to other less excusable diversions from the path of righteousness. Nan's mother, meeting her daughter at the foot of the stairs as the young woman carried cross, tearful, tremulous Davy up to bed, just shook her head. The almost imperceptible movement made itself felt by Mr. Roberts across the width of the hallway; despair settled upon him.

"May I help you wash up since Nan is busy with the little boy?"

"Thank you," Nan's mother said. "Yes, thank you very much. Let me give you a drying-up cloth. I will get my husband to settle your mother by the fire and find her something to look at—would she like some old photographs of Bantwich before the bombing, do you suppose? His parents had quite a collection: and there's a scrapbook of local celebrities and news items he made himself when he was a child."

He began to tidy the piles of used crockery, to separate out silver and cutlery, glass and china; when his hostess came back she gave him a glance of wonder, charged with amusement, and he blushed, he felt himself blushing.

"You're an experienced washer-up," she said, to cover his embarrassment and her wonder.

"I suppose so. There's very little to do at home with

only two of us: it doesn't take long if it's done methodically." Then he said, burning his boats, "I know what you're thinking. You're thinking I'm a proper old maid." And as she began laboriously on a denial, "No, don't. There's no need. I know what I'm like and I'm not specially proud of it. Audrey, my wife, used to loathe it: it didn't bother her, mess and untidiness. It doesn't bother me much, to be honest. But somebody in a home has to care or everything goes to pieces."

She nodded: he thought she was very like her daughter, in colouring, in voice, most of all in manner.

"Yes, I see. If you weren't there, your mother wouldn't look after her home properly."

"She never has. My father had ulcers because she never gave him a meal on time. I ought to have ulcers too I suppose: but I thought I'd rather learn to cook than go through all that just to prove I was a man."

"Mr. Roberts—Rob, is that all right, should I call you that?"

"Please. Nan does."

"Rob, if you were to marry my daughter, should you want her to live with your mother? Perhaps I shouldn't ask you," she went on, in the face of his silence, "because I don't believe that things have gone that far between you. But she might, it's just possible she might ask me what I think, because the other time she didn't ask, and I was too proud to tell her without being asked, and you probably know what happened. This time I want to be ready; if there's even a hint of question I want to know beforehand what I'm going to say."

"Do these cups go on that shelf?" he now asked; his back was turned to her: from his voice she could not tell whether he was annoyed at her impertinence, as he might very well be, both Nan and he being of age, both of them having experience of the married state. And when she had answered yes, and he had put those cups away and turned to face her, she saw that he was not annoyed, he was profoundly wretched.

"I am over forty," he said now, "but I think I might change still, perhaps change a good deal with a young wife and a child or children. Nan isn't far from being a child herself, she will change a lot. My mother won't change, it's no use expecting it. If I married your daughter and we went away to live on our own it would be like a sort of death for her; she has no friends, she won't make any now. She'll get odder and odder and lonelier and lonelier until she dies or goes into a home or a hospital. She's quite well off, she could afford a companion, but nobody wants that sort of work these days and no companion could put up with her week after week. Nan couldn't live in the same house with her, I'm sure of that, especially not with a child; she'd loathe it, she'd end up loathing me. The way I look at it," he said now, and never stopped polishing the milk jug he had long since dried, so that he would not have to look up and meet the woman's eyes, "I've no right to ask Nan to lead that sort of unbearable life. But I don't think I've any more right to leave my mother flat, because she hasn't anybody else. Nan has you and her father and her child, even now: and in a week or a month or a year, with her looks and her charm it couldn't possibly take more than a year, she'll have somebody else to be in love with: I do believe she loves me now," he said. "It doesn't seem right or probable, but I do believe it. But that doesn't mean that she won't sooner or later be glad that she didn't commit herself to anything; glad I didn't actually put her in a spot by asking her to marry me, I mean."

"Yes, I see."

"I expect you think I give up too easily."

"My dear man, what I think doesn't matter. I'll tell you one thing. My daughter doesn't give up easily: she's a fighter, if she needs to be."

"Mrs. Broadbent—"

Something in his tone told her that the subject was changed: his next words still concerned her daughter but the emphasis had shifted, he had subtly contrived to put a distance between them.

"—How much does Nan go out on her own?"

"On her own? Why, virtually never. She does a little local shopping for me in the morning, while my maid's here to take care of Davy, and she takes him to the park in the afternoon—would you call that alone?"

"Does she take the dog?" Mr. Roberts asked, for a large lazy golden retriever had lain upon the hearthrug all through the afternoon; whenever conversation had lagged somebody had found something to say about Janus or whatever the beast was called: in the course of that dismal visit Davy's attention had been drawn to it at least a dozen times, while spoonfuls of scrambled eggs had or hadn't been shoved into his open mouth.

"Yes, always. Why?"

"And at night?"

"Only to your class on a Tuesday. Mr. Roberts—" She had reverted to the formal address, not as a formality; it was plain that, coming from a man who had just more or less announced that he didn't intend to marry her daughter, she regarded this interest in her daughter's movements as distinctly queer. "What right have you to ask these questions?"

He hesitated, but only for a moment.

"She could be in some danger. She's told you—hasn't she?—about this husband of my former wife who's disappeared—and who may have murdered Arthur Hallam and perhaps a young man in Nottingham? What Hal-

lam and that boy have in common is that elegies have
been written for their namesakes. There's an elegy for an
old woman called Ann Jones, written by Dylan Thomas.
It's not as famous as the others but Harvey would know
it. And if he's not quite completely insane, Nan's being
my friend might make him particularly keen on tracking
her down."

"You can't be serious, Mr. Roberts!"

"I'm perfectly serious. The police thought of the same
thing: that people with certain names might be in danger,
and one of the newspapers had a printed list; somewhere
in England there are probably one or two young men
called John Keats and some young woman called
Elizabeth Drury taking extra care not to go out alone in
the dark just at present. But the newspapers didn't
mention Ann Jones: just as well, in a way, there must be
hundreds of them—just as Harvey can't have had much
trouble finding himself an Edward King."

"I see. You really think there's something in it?"

"I'm sure there is."

Their eyes met.

"I don't want to alarm her, Mr. Roberts. She's had a
bad week with Davy's illness; and she's unsettled
anyway, she hasn't been quite herself this past month. I'll
have a word with her father and if she does think of
going out in the evening to a cinema or anything we'll
drive her."

"And if she comes to my class the day after tomorrow
I'll bring her home myself."

After a scarcely perceptible pause Nan's mother said,
"Thank you. Yes, that way we shan't need to worry."

Later that evening, when Mr. Roberts and his mother
had been some time gone and Davy was asleep at last
and Nan was lying in a hot bath trying to forget the
disappointments of the afternoon, Dr. Broadbent after

some minor delays and difficulties succeeded in getting through to Inspector Hunt. They exchanged courtesies: then the good doctor explained why he had called, and the inspector agreed that it was a case, distinctly, for caution. No point in upsetting anybody, but of course a watch must be kept. Nan's father might rest in peace.

CHAPTER ELEVEN

Among the smaller bequests in Professor Hallam's will was one which gave Humphrey Baird and Mervyn Prothero almost equal pleasure. He had left the bulk of his collection of books on the ancient Mediterranean civilisations to the nation, but had excepted those volumes which he had purchased out of the Snettisloe funds or which had been commissioned for the University of Bantwich, under the terms of various Snettisloe Research Fellowships. These would make, in fact, once the will had been proved, quite a substantial addition to the library in the Chambers; and on the Tuesday morning after Mr. Roberts took his mother to tea with Nan's parents Baird had the pleasing task of going round his present stock and deciding how best to accommodate the Hallam bequest, which must clearly have a place of honour on these already overcrowded shelves. Consultation with Miss Carr had revealed a slight divergence of views. Miss Carr had scant patience with the current outbreak of enthusiasm for the social sciences, and favoured moving cultural anthropology, social and industrial psychology and socio-economic theory to the gallery upstairs, even though this would mean endless running up and downstairs for herself and her junior assistants, since the public was kept out of the gallery. Baird, who felt no greater enthusiasm for sociology in general than his second in command, was decidedly less enthusiastic about leg work and thought that one of the less sought after sections—foreign literature, for instance, or philosophy, at present under something of a cloud—might better be moved out to make way for the anticipated influx. Stalemate was reached at about eleven, when they called a truce by tacit consent: Baird turned to their first borrower of the morning and assured Miss Carr with a warmth that concealed some annoyance at her obstinacy that he would cope. The borrower returned the *Collected Poems* of W. B. Yeats and remarked on the beauty of the morning, which up to that moment Baird had failed to notice in his preoccupation with the cussedness of women and the inadequate size of his premises.

"Yes, it's a fine day for November. Here's your ticket, Mr. Peachment, don't you want it?" for Mr. Peachment was already halfway to the door, ignoring the scrap of folded buff-coloured card on the counter.

"Eh? Oh, thank you, no. No, I won't be needing it again."

"Don't you find our library useful?" Baird said, on a note of mild hurt. "There's five weeks of term still to go, you know."

"I'm afraid I shan't be here. I'm off to London in a day or two."

"You're leaving Bantwich?" Baird said, and cursed himself for ever having started this conversation, which promised him no interest and looked like delaying his mid-morning break until there was no point in taking it.

"I've never really been here," Mr. Peachment said, with a rather diffident smile. "I'm travelling around, you see. Footloose and fancy free, you might call me. I've no special ties anywhere, so I decided I might spend the first few months of my retirement moving from place to place till I found where I'd like to settle for the rest of my days. I've lived all my life in one place, and I never much cared for it; so now I've tried the southwest, which is beautiful and warm, but expensive and overcrowded in the summer, and the Isle of Wight, that's the same with hippies added, and London, and East Anglia and now Bantwich."

"You surely never thought of settling down in Bant-wich?" Baird said incredulously. "Most of us who work here can't wait to get out of it!"

"There are worse places, Mr. Baird, believe me there are. I've enjoyed my few weeks here very much. I've had time to look about me and I've met some pleasant people. I've spent a lot of time in the Chambers; it's peaceful, and people are friendly, and I've had a lot of pleasure from my Tuesday evening classes. Very nice ladies and gentlemen in that class, perhaps I should say gentleman, since there's only one beside myself. In all my years of work I never thought I should make a friend of a tax inspector, but we've got on very well, considering all the money he's had off me in my time. No more now, though. I've bought an annuity, my daughter's well set up in life, and I've enough for comfort. That's a very satisfying thought, Mr. Baird, I do assure you. Whether it's long or short I've no need to pinch and scrape."

Baird hid his embarrassment by picking up Mr. Peachment's unwanted ticket.

"And you're sure you won't want this again?"

"Oh, quite sure. You've seen the last of me. Let me wish you all the best."

"Thank you very much," Baird mumbled. "The same to you."

He waited only to see Mr. Peachment safely out of the room before he called one of the juniors to the counter and slipped out of the other door, the one on to the fire escape. The morning was indeed fine, he observed as he ran down two flights of stairs and let himself in through the back door of the main lecture theatre, where he pushed aside the heavy curtains along the window wall and came out at the side of the platform where Professor Hallam had met his death. All this took less than half a minute. It would have been very easy, Baird realised, as Hunt had realised some weeks before, for somebody to use precisely this route to enter the lecture theatre, poison Hallam's drinking water, slip the extra slide into the box and run back upstairs. It wasn't a particularly gratifying thought that a murderer might have done just that; and that a murderer might, on some previous occasion, in the daytime almost certainly when there would likely as not be only one assistant in the library, have rehearsed just that movement: waiting until the assistant was busy with cataloguing or replacing books upon the shelves, and calculating the chances of being seen slipping in or out of that inconspicuous door. Useless to think about it, he told himself as he went through to the main hall, he had already told the police how many people had been in the library the night that Hallam died. Before the evening classes had started Nick Faraday came in to return a book, Roberts to look up a reference, Mr. Peachment took out his Yeats, men and women personally quite unknown to him wandered about, Prothero was in and out like a rabbit, fidgeting over my estimate for the Library Appropriation Fund—and talk of the devil, he thought rather unkindly, for there was Prothero striding over to the enquiries booth; the second post had just come in, and Wilson was sorting it.

"Three for you, Mr. Prothero. Couple of circulars, Mr. Baird. Several for the warden, one for Miss Carr. One for Dr. Faraday."

"I'll take that," Prothero said smoothly. "He won't be coming in again this term. I will check his address with the office and send it on to him."

"You needn't go to all that trouble. I live two doors away from him," Baird said. "I can drop it in on my way home." He held his hand out; he did not doubt for a moment that Prothero would immediately hand over the envelope, a long one, with an official-looking name printed in the upper left hand corner and a London W.1 postmark. But Prothero, far from handing it over, snatched it away; his face darkened, for an extraordinary moment Baird suspected that he had been in danger of having his outstretched hand slapped, as a child's hand might be slapped in the act of refusing to give up something precious to an angry parent. Then Prothero regained control; he even managed a smile.

"Don't put yourself out, Baird. It will be dark by the time you leave the building, it may be pouring with rain, there could be fog or even snow. This is a treacherous month, alas. A fine morning means nothing."

He strutted away in full possession of Nick Faraday's letter, leaving Wilson and Baird not quite looking at each other.

"Very edgy, very jumpy, Mr. Prothero is at the moment, sir. Can't help noticing it. Daresay he needs a holiday."

Term only started a few weeks ago, Baird thought, and though Prothero's a great worrier, he doesn't really suffer from overwork; but Wilson's right just the same. He has been behaving oddly the last few days: that weird business with the picture a week ago—I wondered then if he wasn't a bit under the weather. He went up the main stairs to the refectory: a quick look through the glass doors to satisfy him that Peachment wasn't there and that Miss Carr and Miss Angus were deeply engaged in conversation and he pushed those doors open and fetched a cup of tea from the counter. He was destined not to be left in peace in spite of these precautions; no sooner had he settled himself with the *Critical Quarterly* than a shadow fell over the page, a commanding voice said, "Here, Baird, have you seen this? What price the literary loony, eh?"

Baird looked up from the newspaper that was being held out for his inspection, to the owner of both voice and newspaper—Nick Faraday, whose manner, always brash, now seemed noisier and less appropriate than ever in the face of the nasty item of news he singled out for Baird's attention. Baird said, by way of postponing comment on that news, "By the way, Prothero has a letter for you downstairs; he was going to check on your address for forwarding."

"Can't be anything important if it came here," Faraday said, indifferently. "Well, go on, read it. Not just the headlines."

Since there was no help, Baird read it.

"Well, what do you think?"

"What are you doing here this morning, Nick?"

"Day off. List cancelled, there's been cross infection in one of the theatres, so we're working on half a cylinder till they track it down. Rather lucky for me, gives me a chance to see what's going on in this place."

"Nothing's going on in this place."

"Up at the university then. They'll probably tackle him up there."

"I won't pretend I don't understand you," Baird said, as evenly as he could manage. "You think if Harvey's body has been found or a body that might be Harvey's the police will be renewing their interest in Roberts."

"You do put it tactfully: I should think he'll be helping

them with their enquiries down at city police headquarters any time now, wouldn't you?"

"I've no idea. I don't want to talk about it. I can't think why you're so interested."

"Expert witness, me dear fellow. If anyone wants to know about our friend's murky past, I'm the boy to tell them. And I've never actually attended a trial for murder, ought to be interesting, don't you think?"

"Very. What a pity they've done away with hanging. Public hanging, especially."

"He wouldn't have been hanged anyway," Faraday said, with barely concealed regret, "not even in the bad old days, not with my evidence. I daresay they'll get a fully blown mind-bender to give evidence on his present state; between us we'll get him off quite lightly, if he undertakes to have treatment. Group therapy, that would do him a power of good. Why, he'd even get away from Mummy at last. You've left half your tea," he cried as Baird left him, mumbling something about being short of time. Faraday shrugged his shoulders, drank up the chilly contents of his own cup, folded his newspaper and slipped it into his pocket. As he left the refectory he bumped into Mervyn Prothero coming in. The older man murmured an apology, then saw who had brushed against him and lost his high colour, with such dramatic suddenness that even the imperceptive Faraday saw that something was amiss.

"Is something wrong, Mr. Prothero? Aren't you feeling well?"

"Thank you, I am in perfectly good health. I may have come up the stairs a little too fast."

"Humphrey Baird said you had a letter for me."

"Did he?" Prothero regained his colour, and with it the appearance of a man thinking quickly and to some purpose. "He must have been mistaken. There was an envelope with your name, addressed to the Chambers. However when I took it to my room to arrange for forwarding I realised that it was intended for you only in your capacity as part-time lecturer in this department; in fact it should really go to the organiser of the course you have so kindly assisted us with."

"If you say so. I told old Humph it couldn't be anything important, not in this dear old backwater." And with this quite gratuitous and indeed unconscious insult to the aspirations and achievements of the Extra-mural Department, Faraday would have left had not the deputy warden's sharp eyes, in which wrath had already replaced rapid calculation, lit upon the newspaper in the doctor's pocket, and more especially on the exposed word, the name Harvey.

"One moment, Faraday, might I see your paper?"

"Certainly. Did you know William Harvey's body has been found? Perhaps the dear old backwater's going to get stirred up again, all those suspicious policemen muddying the place up with their big boots. I bet you hated it, I know Dr. Bentley did: my father's his G.P. and he's had the old man on tranquillisers ever since."

Prothero flushed at this indiscretion, but could not let his thoughts dwell for long on the warden's discomfiture, his own being so much more profound, and as he alone knew, so much more reasonably grounded in circumstances. *This discovery,* he read, *will once again focus interest on the Chambers, Bantwich, where only two weeks ago Professor Arthur Hallam was murdered in front of a score of eager seekers after knowledge in the university's Extra-mural Department. Are further murders likely? Scotland Yard's investigators are asking themselves. Was the death of young Edward King one of a series planned by a homicidal maniac with the mind of a brilliant scholar?*

"Brilliant scholar, my eye!" Prothero exclaimed. "Any fool with access to a public library or a few shillings for the *Oxford Book of English Verse* could find 'Lycidas,' and Cowley's elegy on Hervey and 'In Memoriam.' Nothing to it."

"Or crosswords," Faraday said; and when Prothero glared incredulously at him, handing back the newspaper, "Quotations and things. Only time I ever look at a poem, when there's a line of verse for a clue with a word left blank. Then out comes the old *Golden Treasury* and I know I've got six across right at least."

Prothero gave him a withering look at this debasing view of the functions of immortal literature and went off to get himself a coffee. In the downstairs lobby Faraday retrieved his short overcoat from its hook, then realised that he had made a mistake. This coat that closely resembled his own, was indeed identical in cut and material and in the saint's name piously machine-embroidered on its label, already had a newspaper thrust into its pocket; not his own tabloid, but the august daily he had had in mind during his conversation with Prothero: the crossword was on the outside of the folded sheet, and had been done, all except a couple of words—already, at eleven o'clock in the morning!—Faraday noted, with surprise and admiration. And as he found his own garment two pegs farther along and slipped comfortably into it, an elderly man with silvered hair and a quiet, somewhat diffident manner collected the other and preceded Faraday to the door.

CHAPTER TWELVE

"Can't say I like Bantwich any better on a third visit," Superintendent Burnivel remarked to Inspector Hunt at the headquarters of that city's Criminal Investigation Department that same Tuesday morning, "but at least the sun's shining, let's be thankful for small mercies. Tell me how things are moving here and I'll pass on what we've found out at our end. We do find things out, you know; though some people don't seem able to believe it. Dr. Faraday, for instance; he's a real dark horse. You bend your mind on that young man, just remembering he's possibly in a position to have access to dangerous things like cyanide, and that he's responsible for Roberts' fingerprints on Hallam's glass, and then wait till I tell you what he's been up to in his off-duty hours."

"Dr. Faraday? I shouldn't have thought this Eng. Lit. stuff was his cup of tea," Hunt said in surprise.

"It might be and it might not," Burnivel said infuriatingly. "Now, what about Roberts? Have you tackled him yet on his movements the weekend Harvey disappeared?"

"He's coming in this afternoon. I thought you'd want to see him yourself. He's shown no disposition to do a bunk; but one small thing turned up. His girl friend's dad's a bit rattled—it seems that that Welsh poet the BBC made such a fuss of wrote one of these funeral poems about an Ann Jones. Interesting, isn't it?"

"Very." Burnivel chewed this over. "How did her dad find out, then?"

"Well, actually," Hunt said in obvious regret, "it was Roberts who told him, or told the girl's mother anyhow. He said they oughtn't let her go out alone at night. But he thought she shouldn't be told herself, in case it frightened her."

"Did he now? So what advice did you give her father?"

"Just the same really. What worries him is that she's due to attend one of Roberts' own lectures at the Chambers this evening; that's how the two met. Roberts told her mum he'd bring her home but Dad's not too happy about the arrangement."

"I don't know that I am either," Burnivel said, "though between you and me I think we can rule him out here and now."

"Why? He has no alibi for Ted King's murder: he could certainly have killed Hallam. He had good reason to kill Harvey. He might argue that killing Hallam and King as well would make his being found guilty but insane almost a foregone conclusion. A few comfortable years in Grendon Underwood chatting up the do-gooders and he'd be as right as rain."

"You've a lower opinion of psychiatrists than I have if you think they're daft enough to be taken in by that drivel," Burnivel said. "And you're forgetting the girl."

"King and Harvey were dead before he ever met her," Hunt said. "He barely knew her when he poisoned Hallam. Now he's probably regretting the whole thing and he'll try to make sure he doesn't get caught."

"So he warns the girl's mother that she might be in danger—don't tell me that that makes sense. Why should he show everyone that he's knowledgeable about these damn poems?"

"Perhaps he is. Perhaps it's her name that attracted him in the first place."

"Then why let on?" Burnivel shook his head. "If any of young King's pub friends or family or neighbours in Nottingham had recognised his photograph, or if the girl Harvey spent his last evening with noticed him hanging about when they came out of the cinema and went home to her flat, then I'd have to believe that that man could be a murderer. But short of that sort of evidence the other's nothing."

"Harvey did go off with a girl then?"

"Yes. Surprise, surprise. An ex-student of his, living the swinging life in Islington of all places; used to be a respectable working class area when I was a child. Yes, they had a meal, went to see an X film, back to Islington, lovely time, just before midnight he leaves her, never seen alive again. Yesterday morning a commune of hippies or whatever the layabouts are calling themselves this winter broke into a house two streets away that's been shut up for years and years while the owner of that particular terrace waits for the value to go up, and there's William Harvey in a pretty poor state of preservation in the basement. Exit would-be squatters at a run. Our chaps say he's been dead just about as long as he's been lost. Cause of death, as in the case of Ted King, knife between the ribs, done from behind. Instantaneous. Now they're showing our friend's picture to various local residents known to frequent the streets late at night, but between you and me I doubt if they'd recognise their own next-door neighbours. Once an area gets classy people don't know t'other from which."

Having delivered himself of this penetrating bit of sociological observation, Burnivel sat forward in his chair and opened his briefcase, taking out a paper which he passed at once to Hunt.

"This might interest you."

It was the carbon copy of a letter to Professor Hallam, and it bore the name and address of a firm of art dealers, not so well known as some, but of great and growing repute. It was dated April 6, 1970, and the crucial paragraph had been underlined in red ink.

> The canvas we inspected for you bore on one side a painting of a rural Italian scene with men and women in an approximation to quattrocento riding garb, sundry hounds and a wounded stag, executed, you have led us to understand, by your late wife.

Hunt stopped for a moment with a look of perplexity, then realised that Charity Hallam was unlikely ever to have been given to the slaying of innocent animal life in the Umbrian foothills, and was accused of nothing worse than a bit of particularly vivid pictorial storytelling. "Well, get on," Burnivel said impatiently.

> This painting, we can confidently inform you, is of no commercial value whatever at the present time. However in view of the remarks made by Mrs. Hallam shortly before her death and reported to us by yourself as to the great potential value of the work in question, we took the liberty of removing the canvas from the frame and discovered that the reverse was occupied by an early work of the late Georges Rouault, a circus scene, somewhat laboured and uncertain in composition, but unquestionably authentic, and likely to be of considerable interest to collectors of post-Impressionist works. The provenance is open to some question, as you will realise, and if you are able to help us to understand how the work came into your late wife's possession the information may forestall

time-consuming enquiries on this point of possible
buyers and art historians generally.

"Get that?" Burnivel said, as Hunt raised his eyes.
"Now read on." He handed over a second letter, this
time in flamboyant longhand, over the signature of
Arthur Hallam. After a word or two of formal acknowl-
edgment, Hallam went on to say,

> I think I can set your mind at rest over the
> provenance of my Roualt. My wife visited Paris
> many times both before and after the First World War.
> She was a woman of extraordinary taste and discern-
> ment, qualities not perhaps immediately apparent
> even to such a biased observer of her own art as
> myself; she undoubtedly bought this painting know-
> ing very well that it would appreciate in value, and
> concealed it in this way both to exclude its valuation
> for estate duty and to prevent her own family, who
> showed a singular enmity towards her husband, from
> circumventing her natural wish that he should share
> her fortune. I have consulted my solicitor and find
> that I am at perfect liberty to sell it on the open
> market. I shall shortly have the pleasure of asking for
> your advice on some other canvasses of hers which I
> still possess, but her specific reference to this particu-
> lar painting just before she died makes me think it
> unlikely that she tried the same trick twice.

There followed some detailed instructions for the
disposal of the Roualt with an enquiry as to the likely
sum to be expected from a private sale.

"Private, you notice," Burnivel said. "For a chap
whose friends thought him a bit of a show-off the late
professor seems to have kept a good story remarkably
quiet. I daresay he waited to make his killing and have a
good round sum to boast about before he spread the news
around. He'd have had to pay capital gains tax anyway:

but even so, he'd a respectable amount to bequeath when he came to making his will in September."

"There's still no motive for murder," Hunt said gloomily, "except for his children, and we've ruled them out already."

"I'm not so sure," Burnivel said. "Like to see another letter, another copy of a letter? I thought it was worth asking the art dealer johnny if anything like Hallam's canvas had come to him more recently, and he said, yes, there had been another. Mrs. Hallam had given away some of her pictures to friends evidently, and Professor Hallam had told his story to one such friend, whose son wrote to the dealer claiming that his mother had a very fine specimen and he'd bring it down to London for the experts to have a look at. And sure enough on the back of the canvas was a"—Burnivel consulted his notes—"a Derain, a wooded landscape. Not so valuable as the circus scene, but they had no difficulty finding a buyer; though once again the vendor didn't want a public auction, even when it was pointed out that he might get a better price. Anyway a cheque for seven thousand pounds was made out just a day or two ago and posted to Dr. Nicholas Faraday. Here's part of that correspondence."

He handed Hunt some more letters, which Hunt read in mild stupefaction.

"Mind you," Burnivel said, "there's nothing criminal in this transaction. Faraday says Mrs. Hallam gave her painting to his mother; he's at perfect liberty to sell it on his mother's behalf. Only it strikes me as a bit odd that he should sell it only a few days after Hallam's death; always keep an eye out for the incident that seems to be one too many, if you follow me. Faraday here when Hallam died, Faraday making sure we knew all about Roberts and his illness. Time we went a little further into

Faraday's movements on the nights when King and Harvey died."

"Seven thousand pounds," Hunt said. "It doesn't seem a lot to commit a murder for—let alone three murders. And what harm could Hallam do him, even if he did find out somebody else was cashing in on Mrs. Hallam's foresight?"

"If it wasn't just one picture—if Faraday was hoping to sell off a whole lot of them and Hallam might have put in some sort of claim?" Burnivel sighed. "Too far-fetched. Why should Charity Hallam have given his mother a whole gallery full of valuable stuff—and how could Hallam make any claim on them if she had? He wouldn't have had a leg to stand on."

"All the same," Hunt said cautiously, "there is something phoney about this second picture; did you notice Faraday's used writing paper from the Chambers for his letter to the art dealer?"

"What if he has? Hard up, I suppose."

"But he only comes here once in a blue moon. He gives two lectures out of a course of ten this term. He'd be much more likely to use hospital paper if he were hard up—at least he could count on getting a reply at hospital. He hasn't even put his home address on it. If he was selling a valuable painting and expecting a fat cheque, why should he get them to send it here, when he's hardly ever in the place?"

"You're a bright lad, aren't you?" Burnivel said. "So sharp you'll cut yourself one of these days, I shouldn't wonder."

"Just ignoring the facts, sir, and giving way to conjecture: like you warned me against the last time you were here."

Their eyes met. Burnivel made a muffled noise, then stood up with a hand outstretched.

"All right. I know when I'm beaten. Somebody's been taking Dr. Faraday's name in vain. Who?"

"If you could stand a bit more conjecture, sir, I'd suggest somebody working in the Chambers regularly: someone who could count on getting a look at the post there at least once a week."

"Like Roberts?"

"Yes, or more likely one of the regulars. And don't forget the Chambers is full of the Hallam woman's paintings. There was a whopper over the fireplace in the warden's room, the morning after Hallam was killed."

"So there was, a right whopper. Hunt—" Burnivel said with narrowed eyes, "do you remember what that painting was of—if you follow me? Was it another hunting scene? I seem to remember women with no clothes on, but maybe they used to hunt in the nude in those days."

"It wasn't a hunt. I'd have remembered. My name," Hunt said. "That's why I looked at the painting at all. I thought it might be by a namesake of mine. No, it was a sort of spring scene, flowers and things, with a dark old man with hairy legs playing pipes for the ladies to dance to."

"Was it now? Get on the phone to this art dealer chappie and ask him if he can tell you what was on the back of the woodland landscape by Derain."

"Would he remember, do you think? I mean, to him it would just be another bit of amateur junk, wouldn't it?"

"It's worth a phone call," Burnivel said.

"It would be cheaper," Hunt suggested cautiously, "just to go round to the Chambers and see if it's still there."

"And how would you get to see it without letting the cat out of the bag?"

"I'd think of something I urgently wanted to ask the warden."

"Such as what?" Burnivel asked.

"Such as whether the deputy warden was telling the truth when he told Dr. Bentley he only painted in water colours."

"What?"

So Hunt explained, and Burnivel listened; and a little later they both put on their overcoats, for the day though bright was chilly, and walked down the hill in the direction of the Chambers.

The warden and Mr. Prothero were closeted together, Wilson, the porter, told them in the vestibule, and would probably be free within the next half an hour. If the gentlemen cared to wait, there was coffee available in the refectory upstairs.

"We'll wait down here," Burnivel said. A table by the wall held brochures, leaflets, application forms for various courses: on the wall above it, posters were pinned. Three hundred Bantwich poets planned a neighbourhood festival. The local Arts Association, with the aid of the Bantwich City Council, the Snettisloe Trust and the Gulbenkian Foundation, was sponsoring a week of avant-garde drama performed by visiting Poles and Americans and Czechs and the Bantwich Thespians. There were pots on display at the Bantwich Centre for the Domestic Arts, and tapestries woven of stainless steel in the foyer of the Bantwich Playhouse.

"Lively place, Bantwich," Burnivel said, with a devilish scowl. "All done on public money too, you bet."

"There are worse uses for public money," a pleasant voice beside him suggested. Its owner, Inspector Hunt explained, was Mr. Baird, the librarian.

"Oh, Mr. Baird. You were here the night Hallam died. I read your statement. We've a few minutes to spare— might we have a word with you?"

"Is it about the murder? I've nothing to say I haven't said already. I read this morning that William Harvey's body has been found, but I didn't know him, I can't help you."

"Possibly not with our investigations into those two deaths. There's a small side issue where you might be able to throw a little light. Is there anywhere we can talk?"

"There's my room. It's on the first floor."

"Right. You wait down here, Hunt."

Baird led the way upstairs: Miss Carr was at her desk, but excused herself hurriedly.

"I won't sit down," Burnivel said. "I don't believe in wasting time, my own or anybody else's. I want to know if any of your colleagues seems to have had a windfall recently: or conversely, if any of them is known to be particularly hard up."

"If they were, they probably wouldn't mention it to me," Baird said guardedly.

"And if they did you probably wouldn't pass it on to the police," Burnivel said. "I don't think reticence is any sort of virtue when murder and larceny's going on in a place. I think it's a public duty to try to stop such things. That's not advanced thinking, of course, but then places like this wouldn't exist, would they, if outdated people like myself didn't spend our time trying to make sure they're not burned down by vandals? So think about it, and then just tell me what I want to know."

"We're all more or less permanently broke in this place, but we seem to manage from one month's end to the next," Baird mumbled.

"No betting men? No heavy gamblers? No one with heavy expenses on the side? Women? Fast cars?"

"This is an Extra-mural Department," Baird said, recovering some of his dignity with his good humour. "You never saw a quieter, more sober set of men and women. We haven't a Jaguar or a Lotus between us, and most of us are honourably domestic. Ten Premium Bonds would be as near to gambling as most of us ever come."

"I see." Burnivel seemed depressed by this general paucity of vice, but tried, though discouraged, another tack. "Leaving money out of it, has any of your colleagues been behaving oddly in the last few weeks—out of character?"

"I don't think so. Dr. Bentley's been rather unwell, he was upset by the publicity over Hallam's death, but he seems better now."

"How about the other one?" Burnivel said, and seeing the change on Baird's face that the librarian was too transparent a man to conceal quickly enough, "the deputy warden, Prothero. Has he been unwell?"

"Not as far as I know."

"Just his usual self?"

"I think so." But Baird did not think so, and the fractional hesitation that stamped him as habitually truthful even now when he was actually lying sounded like a trumpet in Burnivel's experienced ears.

"Do you, Mr. Baird? Or do you just prefer to think so?" And when Baird said nothing but changed colour, Burnivel followed up his advantage. "Think again, Mr. Baird. You've noticed something, and naturally you'd rather not talk to me about your colleague. Maybe it'll help if I tell you that we haven't at the moment any reason at all to connect Mr. Prothero with the death of Mr. Harvey and the young man in Nottingham. We know that he spent a little time in the lecture theatre here with Professor Hallam and that he certainly had an opportunity to poison the drinking water, the best chance anybody had, most likely. There's just a chance that he may have had a motive for killing Hallam; if he did, it will be connected with a painting by the professor's wife."

Nobody could have missed Baird's agitation now. He sat down as if the strength had gone out of his legs. Ten minutes later Burnivel was in possession of the salient facts of that extraordinary visit Miss Blount and Baird had made to the warden's room, when the spring scene was said to have fallen from its place; when the window had been wide open, and Prothero's fingers had been smeared with—what?

"Paint, obviously," Burnivel said. "My friend Hunt tells me the deputy warden's an amateur painter himself. My guess is that he copied the picture in Dr. Bentley's room—not too difficult to do, given the communicating door. Then he replaced the original with his copy and sent if off to London for valuation."

There was a tentative knock at the door and Miss Carr came in.

"Oh, I'm sorry, I thought the inspector had gone."

"I'm just going," Burnivel said. "You'd better come down with me now, Mr. Baird. We'll see Mr. Prothero at once and get this cleared up."

"There was a ticket lying on the library counter, Mr. Baird. One of the juniors asked me what you wanted doing with it. Should we send it to the borrower or wait and see if he calls for it?"

"Didn't I throw it out?" Baird said. "It belongs to that nice old chap Peachment from Roberts' class. He's leaving Bantwich, he tells me. He won't need it any more."

"What name did you say?" Burnivel asked; a man

who seemed generally wound up like a clock spring, his state of tension now passed over from the mechanical to the galvanic.

"Peachment," Baird repeated, wondering. "He's retired, I believe, moving around the country looking for somewhere to settle down. Don't know what could have made him think of trying Bantwich, but he isn't staying, evidently: I supposed he might turn up tomorrow night."

"Where can I find him?"

"They'll have his address in the office. But what about the deputy warden?" Baird said, for whatever was in Burnivel's mind now it was nothing Baird had intentionally placed there.

"Oh, Mr. Prothero. He can wait. I'm much more interested in your nice old chap."

Mr. Peachment had taken lodgings in a humble but decent street of red brick Victorian houses, within a mile of the main railway line to London. When Hunt and Burnivel arrived there the house was empty. They made enquiries among the neighbours who assured them that Mrs. Page was unlikely to be away for long; they had seen her go out with her shopping bag soon after eleven, and yes, one of them had seen her lodger leave too, with a small suitcase and a holdall, a little earlier, perhaps about ten. There was nothing to be done but wait: Burnivel went back to the police car—for what he had to do now was too urgent for footwork—and arranged for a watch to be kept on Bantwich City station and its left luggage department and for more men to be sent to the intercity bus terminal. So far, he was thankful to know, Bantwich had no airport.

Then a woman of fifty crossed the road towards them, her expression showing some wonder, perhaps alarm. She had been crying, her face was red and puffy. She carried a plastic shopping bag, which was clearly empty: she saw them looking at it and burst into tears. "My cat," she sobbed. "Found him this morning in the tropical fish tank. I've just taken him off to the vet's. The neighbours said to put him in the rubbish, but it doesn't seem right and the bin men wouldn't like it, it's a week before they come again."

"Never mind your cat," Burnivel said roughly. "We're police officers, madam, and we came here for a word with your lodger, Mr. Henry Peachment. Can you tell us where to find him?"

Fresh tears welled up. "He's gone too: gave me notice this morning, two weeks' rent, very regretful to have to leave in such a hurry." She opened her front door. "Come in, won't you? Don't mind the mess, I've been too upset to tidy up. He was over fourteen, mind, I said to the vet. I've been thinking for weeks he ought to be put down, but he's a sort of companion for me, you get used to a cat around the place."

"Could you show us the room Mr. Peachment used to occupy, madam?" Burnivel said, stifling his impatience.

"I'm sure there's been some mistake," she wailed. "You can't tell me Mr. Peachment's done anything he shouldn't. He's a lovely clean gentleman, so clever too, always telling you things out of books and sitting down quietly to do the crossword during 'Coronation Street.' I don't know how he could concentrate but he never once asked me to turn it off."

"What did Mr. Peachment say," Hunt said, under some compulsion of recent memory that helped him to ignore Burnivel's scowl, "when you told him your cat was dead?"

"He smiled ever so kindly; he said, did I know the same thing once happened to a poet's cat. And when he came downstairs to say good-bye he gave me a little bit of paper. 'It's an epitaph for Tibbles,' he said. Oh, how empty the house is going to be tonight without them!'' She fumbled in her pocket and brought out her handkerchief and Mr. Peachment's kind thought. "Here it is; I don't like to be rude but it wasn't suitable, Tibbles never went near that tank before."

Hunt took the slip of paper from her and showed it to Burnivel; this time the typed quotation was exceedingly brief:

What cat's averse to fish?

CHAPTER THIRTEEN

Mr. Roberts counted up the loose change in his pocket, found that it was probably enough for his needs and pushed open the door of the public call box in the vestibule of the Chambers. Barsted, the porter, had told him a moment before that the warden would like a word with him; Mervyn Prothero had pushed past him, evidently on his way out of the building, looking curiously crumpled, an older man than his years. These two small oddities in the odd world he seemed at the moment to inhabit hardly impressed him at all, whereas a few weeks before a sudden urge on Dr. Bentley's part to waste time on a mere casual lecturer would have set him speculating furiously, and such a change in Prothero's appearance and demeanour would not have slipped his mind in the few seconds it took him to find out the dialling code for Cambridge, and listen to the sounds summoning Audrey to her telephone.

"Greg?" She sounded incredulous. "Where are you? Where are you calling from?"

"Bantwich. I'm at the Chambers. I tried to write to you, I wrote two letters last night and then tore them up."

"You're *free!*" Now he understood the incredulity, or partly understood it; he was surprised to find how angry that made him.

"Of course. Why shouldn't I be?" There was a pause; clearly, outspoken though she had always been, actually to utter the words, "I thought you would have been arrested for the murder of my husband," was beyond her powers. "I wanted to tell you that I am sorry."

"Sorry!" she breathed.

"Yes. A few years ago I couldn't have said that, even in the way of politeness. But now it's the simple truth, I am honestly sorry. It seems such a waste. I said a lot more than that in the letters, but then I decided I ought to speak to you. I ought to know how you are."

"I'm all right," she said at last. "I knew, you know, almost at once. That evening I rang you, in my heart I knew." After another silence, she said brightly, "I expect you had an alibi, then, for the night Bill was killed."

"No, I didn't. There's just the small point that I didn't do it. I can't prove that I wasn't in Islington that night, but then nobody can prove that I was. The police are being very reasonable. It's all very unlike what you'd expect a murder investigation to be, very quiet and businesslike. I spent two hours yesterday with the man from Scotland Yard and by the end of it I couldn't believe that I'd ever known Bill, that he was ever a real person, let alone that I'd ever hated him."

"He doesn't seem real to me, either," that man's widow said. Then she added, "I went down to London to identify the body."

"My God. I never thought of that."

"It was bad." Her voice was steady. "You'd have thought that girl's identifying him would have been enough, but apparently it wasn't. I went to see her afterwards: the funny thing was I knew her quite well. She was one of Bill's students about six years ago. He'd been going to her on and off ever since."

"I'm sorry."

"Yes, well, it was no surprise to me. First thing I saw when I walked into her flat was an enlargement of that snap I took of you and Bill, the day you went over to Haverhill fishing. Seems he must have had her neatly stowed away for his convenience before I married him." Now her voice shook: for a moment Roberts felt a powerful urge to reach along all those miles of telephone cables and caress her, but her next words put that urge where it belonged with all the other quixotic impulses of his that at one time or another she had blasted with her icy ridicule. "You have to hand it to Bill, he'd never let himself be left high and dry like you, Greg dear. And the silly bitch seems to have thought their squalid little affair was the great love thing of the century. She'd given up everything for him, run away from home, her mother had died of grief or high blood pressure, she didn't seem to know which, she'd had row after row with her dear old dad, who'd worshipped the ground she walked on, she'd seen him looking at Bill on the banks of the Stour just like Donna Whatnot's father must have looked at Don Giovanni—anyway I soon rubbed the romantic gloss off, I can tell you."

"I'm sure you did."

"She had to grow up sometime. I'd got over all that girlish nonsense even before I married you, Greg."

"Or you wouldn't have married me."

"Exactly. Anyway I left her in no doubt where she stood and what a lot of excellent company she stood in. Why, I told her, if I had to go up and down the country drying the tears of all Bill's ex-mistresses, I'd need a mileage allowance."

Mr. Roberts said nothing: there seemed to be nothing to say.

"Greg? Are you there, Greg?"

"Yes, I'm here."

"Thank you for ringing."

"It seemed the very least I could do."

Since she had been willing to assume, not five minutes before, that he had done the most, the very most, a jealous man would be capable of, he could not help but admire her self-possession as she thanked him again for going to so much trouble, and rang off. How could I have married her, how could I have loved her, how could I have minded, even a little, when he took her from me? Mr. Roberts asked himself, and left the phone booth for Dr. Bentley's room, those fruitless questions leaving him forlorn. The warden was not alone, Humphrey Baird was with him.

"Mr. Roberts, I cannot thank you enough for sparing me some of your precious time. We have had some very sad, some very sad and disturbing news; Baird here knows all about it. Of course there is no question of prosecution; we shall all keep the matter entirely quiet. Fortunately the police assure us that Prothero's unfortunate lapse is in no way connected with the other strange and terrible events of the past few weeks, though it might never have come to notice had they not been so thorough in their investigations. That is so, is it not, Baird?"

"Yes, Warden."

Mr. Roberts looked from one man to the other in mild wonder, but knew better than to try to rush Dr. Bentley.

"Prothero tells us that it was entirely on behalf of the Extra-mural Department, entirely for our benefit that he embarked upon this extraordinary course of deceit and duplicity. It seems he had become a little obsessed with the present administration's decision to cut back the funds available for adult education. Professor Hallam mentioned to him in strictest confidence some while ago that his late wife's paintings were sometimes painted upon the backs of valuable masterworks: he accordingly prepared a copy of her Persephone dancing to the Pipes of Pan and replaced the original in my room with it, sending that canvas to London for valuation and sale. The Derain on the back brought him in a considerable sum, which he proposed, he tells us, unobtrusively to pay over to this department as a gift from an anonymous well-wisher. Only a few moments ago he left a cheque with me for a very considerable sum."

Mr. Roberts caught Baird's eye. He then looked at the cheque Dr. Bentley was waving gently before him.

"But that cheque's signed Nicholas Faraday."

"No, it was signed by our deputy warden in Dr. Faraday's name. He opened a bank account in that name in one of the suburban branches where neither of them is known, and had the purchaser of the painting, which he claimed to be the property of Dr. Faraday's mother, pay the purchase money into that account. He was eager, as you see, to conceal his identity. He did not want his left hand to know what his right hand was doing."

"I can understand that," Mr. Roberts said with feeling. "So the painting over your fireplace isn't an original Charity Snettisloe?"

"No; first of all he signed it C.S. All her other paintings in this building are signed in that way, since most of them were painted in her girlhood. Then he realised that this was a late work and should have her husband's initial; he could hardly check with the original, since he had already sent it off to London. So he decided he must risk changing it before the mistake was realised. Miss Blount and Baird here caught him in the act, and Miss Blount knew at once that there was something amiss—she had seen the picture signed, and knew that on that occasion Mrs. Hallam, unused to her new status, had used the wrong initial."

"Prothero says that he felt the mere fact Mrs. Hallam left this painting here and never gave it to her husband, although it concealed a fine original, suggests that she was making the department a secret gift."

"I think we should charitably assume that he is right on that point," Dr. Bentley said, "and in that light I think we must now arrange for all the other paintings to be taken down and inspected."

Baird and Mr. Roberts exchanged glances.

"With a view to cashing in on their market value if they happen to be worth something?"

"Not at all. With a view to turning them the other way round and attracting a steady stream of wealthy and influential visitors to the Chambers. There is no need," Dr. Bentley magnificently declared, "for us to cry our wares in the marketplace, but equally there is no need for us to hide our light under a bushel. Now, Mr. Roberts, you may be wondering why I should wish to let even so discreet a member of our associate staff as yourself become party to this mildly scandalous affair. You may well ask yourself, why does the warden, who must be aware that I have other pressing matters on my mind at this moment, seek to divert me with gossip about his unfortunate deputy? There is a reason, I assure you. Mr. Prothero is, let us all be thankful, sufficiently near retirement age for his premature departure to need no explanation; he himself has given me to understand that he feels much in need of a rest after the stress and strain of the last weeks. He feels, and what is more to the point, I feel, that a younger man who has already rendered this department valuable service should have the opportunity of helping to direct the department's course in the seventies, under, ahem, the guidance of my more experienced self. In other words, Mr. Roberts, I feel I should just convey to you the possibility of our considering with very great favour any application you might think of putting forward for the position of deputy warden, when it becomes vacant, as it shortly will."

"Why?" Mr. Roberts asked Baird five minutes later, when they were alone in Baird's room. "Why me?"

"Well, believe it or not, I think old Bentley knows a good deal about what goes on in this place, despite all the evidence to the contrary. He knows you're a favourite with the regular customers, he thinks you've had a raw deal lately, he knows you wouldn't be likely to—would it be libellous to call what Prothero's been doing, diverting public monies?—anyhow you wouldn't be likely to follow his example."

"I'm not so sure. For weeks now a woman who knew me for years has been sure I've committed murder; for weeks now I've been sure a man I once knew well committed murder. Now we hear that a decent, hard-working man has risked imprisonment for a few thousand pounds. I can't feel certain of anything just now."

"Well, whatever basic criminal proclivities I may have I know one thing that'd keep me straight—the fear of being found out. You're early, aren't you?"

They were standing under the clock in the main hall, which prompted Baird's change of subject; though he would have changed it anyway, seeing that his friend was in no mood to make light of the situation.

"Yes," Roberts now said. "I'm meeting Nan for a drink before the class. Will you join us?"

"Wouldn't I be in the way?"

"That's the idea, roughly. It won't do, you see."

"Won't it?"

"No. For me, probably. But not for her. I'd be sixty when she's forty. And that's the smallest part of it." After a moment Mr. Roberts said, as if it were his turn to change the subject, "I shall have to disappoint Dr.

Bentley. My mother's longed to move south for years and years, she dreads each winter more than the last. I thought of looking for a post at Exeter or Bristol or one of the new universities."

"Couldn't you find Mrs. Roberts a nice hotel at Bournemouth or Torquay and visit her two or three times a year?"

"Is that what you'd do in my shoes?"

"Yes," Baird said, without hesitation.

"It wouldn't shorten those twenty years."

"It would, in a way."

"It's not comfortable," Mr. Roberts said, "despising oneself, and knowing the only way to stop it means hurting somebody else very much."

"When the somebody else ought, in the course of things, to expect this particular hurt?"

Mr. Roberts shook his head. "Don't think I don't know all the sensible rationalisations. There'd be no problem if I didn't."

"Go and have a drink with Mrs. Jones. Try to see it her way. After all, she's as much involved in this as you and your mother."

"I doubt it. Though she thinks so just now."

"I can't understand you," Nan said, putting her drink down on the bar with a noisy splashing movement. "If I tell you I love you and want to marry you and I'm willing to take a chance on getting on with your mother and I'm not your wretched Audrey, or whatever her name was— why can't you believe me?"

"I believe you. I'm sure you're telling the truth. But what's true today won't be true in six months' or a year's time. You know, you must know, after last Sunday, that you couldn't bring up your child, or our children if we have any, under the same roof as my mother."

"She won't live forever," Nan said brutally, but with a childlike pout that almost prevented his recoil. And he covered that instantaneous distaste with a sort of joke, saying, "They do live forever, women like my mother. And they need more and more attention as they get older. You couldn't do it. I won't ask you to."

She drained her glass and slid off her stool by the bar.

"Come on, then. Come and chat up all the other old dears. I daresay you feel safer with them than you do with me."

She would not wait a moment for him, pushed open the door of the pub for herself, strode out into the chill and the dark. He raced after her, surprising himself by his own turn of speed: he thought, he could not be sure, that in the shadows along the side wall of the building something or someone moved. He thought, he was sure, that the tall man elaborately fumbling with his pipe in the lee of the house on the corner was one of Hunt's men watching out for Nan, as he was watching. He caught up with the girl at the steps of the Chambers, he was in time to push those heavy doors open, but she swept in with her face averted and made a bee-line for the ladies' cloakroom. He found her silly petulance almost as delightful as it was saddening. It convinced him that he was right, that he could never now possibly stand in any relation to her more intense than that of teacher to pupil. After those few seconds of near panic outside the pub, mere sadness was quite bearable. He hung up his coat and went into the lecture theatre, familiar faces beaming at him. Since he was there, since Harvey was known to be dead and he was still there, his class might choose whether to believe him innocent or the police remiss; these seemed to be simple alternatives, of which they greatly preferred the first; for how could they believe that a man whose feet might even now be warmed by socks

lovingly knitted by their own hands, last year or the year
before, on just such chilly evenings as this leading up to
the last class before Christmas, the gay greeting, the
murmured thanks—how could one believe in the terrible
wickedness of such a man? Mrs. Berg, Miss Blount,
Mrs. Landor, Mr. Bell—although his experience in the
Inland Revenue inclined him to a darkish view of human
nature—knew their tutor through and through; his
scruples, his compunctions were as obvious to them as
the size of his shoes and his preference for sober hues
and simple patterns. He met their kind eyes, their
concerned glances; they all knew from their extensive
reading that guilty men could face no such ingenuous
looks, or could face them only with a bold malignant
stare. Even the boldest villain could not, they felt,
encounter the gaze of Sister Marie Louise without
flinching. This test he passed. They settled back with a
ripple of satisfied sighs, a rustle of notepads. Mrs.
Landor said brightly, loudly, "Are we going on with *The
Moonstone* this week, Mr. Roberts?" and received
grateful acknowledgement from the rest of the class,
who envied her assurance almost as much as they
admired the generous spirit that informed it. She made it
possible for him to produce a smile, to say, "Good
evening," in an ordinary tone. And after they had
chorused back a greeting he said, in Mrs. Landor's
general direction, "Yes, I thought tonight we would take
Wilkie Collins as a useful jumping-off ground. You'll
have seen, some of you, Dorothy Sayers' introduction to
the Everyman edition of this book, and the tribute she
pays him for his scrupulous fairness, for the way in
which he makes every fact necessary for the solving of
his mystery available to the reader right from the
beginning. There's no reason whatever why every one of
us shouldn't know the identity of the thief at the end of

Gabriel Betteridge's narrative. But did any of you know, if it was the first time you had read the book?''

Mostly they did not; though Mr. Bell claimed that a natural mistrust of philanthropists had coloured his own choice of likely culprit.

"I didn't want to know," Miss Blount said. "They were all such good characters, such nice solid people. I would rather the Moonstone had been stolen by a magpie or something. I'm sure I have seen somewhere that a magpie did once steal a valuable jewel and a poor girl rather like Rosanna Spearman, you know, was very nearly hanged for it. Though of course the thief in this book wouldn't have been hanged, would he? The Victorians were not so barbarous.''

"Nobody is hanged for anything these days," Mr. Bell said, and then blushed, for the ladies were not pleased at this tasteless interjection, worse than tasteless in the circumstances, and hastened to cover it up with hurried exploratory queries about whatever Miss Blount could have had in mind?—one lady, who turned out to have sung coloratura parts with the Bantwich Amateur Operatic Group, triumphantly traced the reference back to Rossini's *Gazza Ladra*, even singing them a bar or two of the unfortunate heroine's music, by way of establishing authenticity. Mr. Roberts stood by his desk while this went on, not knowing whether to laugh or to cry, and wondering if that widespread view of human life as only finding fulfilment in passionate sexual love, sublimated in the raising of a family, was not altogether too narrow, too rigid: what puritans we are, he considered, to reject out of hand such smaller loyalties, such forbearances, such impulses of tender feeling! And when finally their faces were again turned to him with a drained look, so much virtue having been put forth on his behalf, he managed for their sakes quite a cheerful, "Now then!

Back to the work in hand! Am I right in thinking that most of you probably didn't even try to solve the mystery—you just settled back to enjoy the masterly storytelling?"

They agreed: from here on his way was clear. He traced the divergence, in his view, of the story that was basically a conundrum—with only the scantiest top-dressing of character and motivation, with only the lightest passing tribute paid, for instance, to the emotions likely to be felt by murderers and their victims, innocent suspects, detectives who were presumptively human, though they functioned virtually as computers—from the novel in which a violent act or acts or a major piece of dishonesty—like the concealment of a will, so favourite a device in the novels of Ivy Compton-Burnett—served only to focus attention on certain intolerable strains in human relationships, or to throw into powerful relief just those aspects of human nature generally kept battened well under hatches. "We shall be reading *Crime and Punishment* next," he told them, "and moving into a genre very popular and perhaps very significant in our own day. But I don't want to go too far along those lines. I want to start soon on the sort of story that sprang directly from the soil ploughed by Wilkie Collins, the puzzle story, where beating the detective to the solution is half the fun of the thing."

Then Miss Blount asked a question about Sergeant Cuff, and another lady wanted reassurance on Collins' handling of police procedure, and Mr. Bell, recovered from his recent rough handling, enquired, with the virtuous air of one who had done his homework, whether, by the strict criteria adduced by Elizabeth Bowen for relevance in the detective novel, the whole Ezra Jennings episode wasn't really to be regarded as so much padding? Ah, who could say when exactly padding became local colour, atmosphere, solidity? If we go back, for instance, to Balzac, where every detail of the Parisian lodging house where old Goriot dies has a documentary reality that breathes unassailable life into the characters—Mr. Roberts pulled himself expertly back, finding himself alone in Paris and feeling even less inclined than usual to desert his class after their goodness to him. Besides, it was time for a break; and he had to know where Nan was. In the hallway outside he caught a glimpse of Inspector Hunt, muffled up in a scarf and an unlikely fur hat, and was reassured. Before he drank his coffee he telephoned her number. Her mother's voice said, yes, she had come in ten minutes ago and gone straight to bed, pleading tiredness. Was anything wrong? "No, nothing is wrong. She didn't come to my class; I just wanted to be sure that she'd got home safely." He waited a moment to get his voice under control. "Give her my love. I probably won't be seeing her again." He rang off quickly, and got back to the lecture room before the ladies. Mr. Bell was already in his place, so were the nuns. Sister Marie Louise and Sister Philomene had been joined by a third of their kind, in a rather different habit, black in colour, more conventional of style; a tall woman with finely chiselled features and dark-rimmed library glasses. She sat a little apart from the others, but was presumably an acquaintance of theirs joining the course rather late in the term, and indeed rather late in the evening, but newcomers often assumed that classes began at eight o'clock and then hesitated to come in before the coffee break. Mrs. Landor and her friends filed in; Mr. Roberts registered the fact that Mr. Peachment had evidently dropped out; indeed, now he came to think of it he had noticed earlier on that Mr. Bell was on his own now, and therefore unlikely to last out the term. The extra nun would at least keep the numbers up. He supposed he had better start worrying about the numbers, since Prothero would worry no longer.

Humphrey Baird was making a perfunctory attempt to tidy his desk before going along to the library and locking up for the night when Superintendent Burnivel knocked on his door, and came in immediately upon his knock.

"Look at this."

This was a bit of paper on which a few words were scrawled.

"What is it?" Burnivel demanded. "Where does it come from? Quick, this isn't a game."

"'*Soldier, statesman, poet he, And all he did done perfectly.*' It's Yeats. It's from his elegy for his patroness' son: 'The Irish Airman,' he wrote that one for him too, it's in all the anthologies."

"Damn the anthologies. What was the chap's name?"

"Gregory. Major Robert Gregory."

"Was it now?" Burnivel was already halfway out of the door.

"That man Peachment," Baird called after him. "He brought back a volume of Yeats the other day."

Burnivel turned in the doorway. "He'd finished with it. We spent a fair part of yesterday afternoon and this morning going through his digs with a fine-tooth-comb. His landlady told us he'd given her notice, paid two weeks' rent, and gone off before lunchtime. His typewriter went, too. She says he often did a little typing in the evening. I had two chaps going round the junk shops and auction rooms all day, and an hour ago one of them ran it down—a student bought it at lunchtime. There were a few sheets of unused paper in the pocket inside the lid, and one of them had those words typed on it over and over; he must have gone on until he got it right.

There was a two-inch strip missing off the sheet. Maybe he's already posted it; maybe he's already God knows where, looking for a Robert Gregory like he looked for an Edward King."

Baird said in a queer voice, "He won't have gone far. There's Mr. Roberts. We call him Rob, but his first name's Gregory."

"Where would he be now?"

"In the lecture room downstairs. Barsted might know if Peachment's here."

"He can't be. I had two men downstairs. One followed Mrs. Jones home. Hunt's there."

"Has any of them ever seen Peachment?"

Burnivel shook his head. "They've the landlady's description."

"He's not very striking," Baird said. "Just a nice-looking older man. He could have slipped in."

They were, almost without knowing how they got there, at the head of the stairs, they were on the first flight down, over the balustrade they could see the ladies of Mr. Roberts' class, coming out in pairs, with laughter. Mr. Bell came with them; Baird shook his head as Burnivel glanced sideways at him. Impossible to believe there could be crude physical danger in this place, he thought, but remembered with sick intensity the sight of Hallam's contorted face and half ran, half slid, down the second flight. Through the open doors they could see Mr. Roberts alive and well, and in conversation with a nun. "Sister Marie Louise," Baird gasped in relief, but even as he said her name he caught out of the corner of his eye a whisk of ankle-length grey skirts in the passageway to the ladies' cloakroom.

The second part of the evening passed quickly. Now that he need not worry about Nan, not at any rate for the present, Mr. Roberts could give his mind fully to the subject, and his class agreed later that they had never seen him so animated. Several of them came up to the desk at half past nine to thank him for a splendid evening. They put their copies of *The Moonstone* back into the box regretfully, they went off with Dostoievsky and a frightened sense of anticipation. At last Roberts was alone; he glanced down the register and put a cross by Nan's name for this date and another by Mr. Peachment's. A shadow fell across the page; he glanced up. The third nun stood there, smiling. He noticed the well-shaped mouth, the slight fuzz over the upper lip, and looked quickly away in case she were not far enough above the vanities of this world to meet his scrutiny without embarrassment.

"Did you enjoy the class? Will you be coming again?"

She said nothing; he wondered if there were female Trappists. Sister Marie Louise might be able to help, but when he looked across the room she was already by the door, he did not like to call her back. Instead he said, "May I have your name, Sister, if you will be coming regularly?" Then, in gentle desperation, "Perhaps you would rather write it down yourself? Have you a pen?"

He turned the register towards her. She fumbled in the voluminous folds of her gown; he was thankful that at least she understood what he wished her to do. He was still quite unalarmed when he saw that what she had drawn out from between those black folds shone like a splinter of glass. He left her to sign her name, went over to the book box and knelt down to lock it. Something knocked him hard under the left shoulderblade, so hard that he pitched forward over the box and struck his chest on the sharp edge of the lid. Then there were voices in the room behind him and the sound of blows. He tried to get up but hands held him. Inspector Hunt, with his Russian cap knocked sideways, told him to stay where he was, he caught a single horrifying glimpse of Humphrey Baird lying on top of the nun, who threshed and struggled and groaned but could not escape because he had her pinned down by her heavy skirts. For the last time in his life Mr. Roberts doubted his sanity—surely this was hallucination! But then his own body began to send strange signals to his wavering mind, he felt sticky wetness over his left flank and his breath came painfully and felt as if it might not come at all. He lay on his side; Hunt, with his Russian hat, was talking across his body to men in uniform, not policemen, though there were policemen in the room now too, and they were disgracefully engaged in helping Baird keep the nun on the floor. Burnivel loomed up with a lean, domestic knife in his hand, sharpened to a fantastic point. "Probably the same one he used for Harvey and King," he said.

"But why me?" Roberts asked, with great difficulty. "Why me?"

"You shouldn't talk, Mr. Roberts," Burnivel said. "He'll tell us all about it later, I shouldn't wonder. He had this bit of paper on him, he put it on your register—one of those fancy messages like he made out for your friend Harvey. '*Soldier, statesman, poet he, And all he did done perfectly.*' Flattering, huh? My God," he said to the ambulance man, "the poor blighter's choking—can't you do something?"

But Mr. Roberts was not choking: he was laughing. The sound of his laughter was the last thing he heard before he lost consciousness.

"I'll tell you what I can," Baird said to Nan Jones on the phone at lunchtime the next day, "I'd have rung before but I've been with Hunt and Burnivel most of the morning. Rob was so taken with the idea that you were in danger because of the Dylan Thomas poem that he never thought of the Yeats—he wouldn't have anyway, it's a marvellous thing, but not very apposite for poor old Rob."

"Why not?"

"Go and look it up when you have a chance. Robert Gregory was the son of Yeats' patroness so I expect he was laying it on with a trowel, but even so he does seem to have been a remarkable chap."

"Rob is a remarkable chap," Nan said coldly. "Have I got it right? You're actually telling me that the police knew this man was a dangerous criminal, this time yesterday, and they still let him get into the Chambers?"

"They couldn't find him. Not very surprisingly; he'd hired a nun's habit from a theatrical costumier's in London weeks ago, and brought it to Bantwich with him; when he left his digs yesterday morning he got on to an early train with his holdall, changed in the toilet and came straight back, leaving his case and holdall in the left luggage; the police were there, but they were looking for the elderly father of the girl Harvey'd been keeping in Islington. Peachment himself doesn't seem to have been sure which of the two was her lover, Harvey or Rob. She had a photograph of the pair of them, taken in the days when Rob hadn't a beard and Harvey had. When the old man retired he seems to have brooded over the waste of his daughter's talents—he'd hoped for such a brilliant future for her, never having had the education he deserved himself. So he killed Harvey and tried to throw suspicion on Rob, in case he was her lover too."

"What will happen to him now?"

"He'll be brought to trial, he isn't unfit to plead. They think he must have got the cyanide to kill Hallam when he was working as a pharmacist, which is a point against his being insane, the police say, because it looks like cool premeditation. But he may have meant it for Harvey. He made a mistake right at the beginning, you see—he hid Harvey's body too well; he came to Bantwich, he sent the message to Harvey's wife, and nothing happened to Rob, he wasn't arrested. So he went on to Hallam and to Edward King. They've found a girl in a branch of a big chemist's in Nottingham who's prepared to swear he brought in that picture of a hawk and a rabbit to get a slide made the very day the local paper there announced the boy's win on the Premium Bonds and printed a picture of him with his pals at the pub he went to every night, including the night Peachment was waiting for him outside."

"I can't feel sorry for him," Nan said. "Even if he hadn't tried to kill Rob, I'd still think he was a monster. Two innocent people, two men who'd never done him a scrap of harm—oh, surely he's mad?"

"Yes, I think so too. I think once he let his hatred for Harvey boil over he couldn't stop himself. Perhaps he wanted to get his own back on the sort of people he thought had ruined his daughter's life, perhaps he even believed he was using their own weapons. There's an awfully trite saying about a little learning being a dangerous thing, and there's a wretched dead cat in a vet's incinerator somewhere in Bantwich to prove it. It's a good thing Prothero can't hear me." There was so long a silence at the end of the line that he thought she must have gone away and he was just about to put the receiver down when she said in a queer way, "Will he be all right, Rob, I mean? I don't care about Peachment."

"Yes, they think so. He had pints and pints of blood dripped into him and some fancy sewing done, but Peachment only got in the one blow. He needed three or four stabs to do for the others."

"Shall I go and see him? He more or less gave me the brush-off last night."

"Did he?" Be careful, Humphrey Baird's conscience told him; don't interfere. You might regret it all your life, they might regret it, they might blame you. "He didn't want to, I'm sure of that. He's fearfully scrupulous, you know. People think it's weakness but it isn't. It's being able to get inside somebody else's skin and know how much they'll suffer."

"Why won't he get inside mine, then?" she demanded.

"Don't ask me that, ask him."

"I'll go now. I'll go right away. I'll make him marry me, you see if I don't."

"You probably will too," Baird said, but she had already rung off, she was already finding her coat, touching up her face, snatching her handbag, shouting to her mother that Davy could go down for his nap now, she'd be back in time to give him his tea, slamming the front door, running down the path, dirtying the hem of her long orange coat again, in such a hurry she was still wearing her oldest shoes, the ones she used to slop around the house in.

Attention Mystery and Suspense Fans

Do you want to complete your collection of mystery and suspense stories by some of your favorite authors? Raymond Chandler, Erle Stanley Gardner, Ed McBain, Cornell Woolrich, among many others, and included in Ballantine's new Mystery Brochure.

For your FREE Mystery Brochure, fill in the coupon below and mail it to:

TA-94